A tragedy of riches by Tony Cointreau is a captivating story of beauty, ambition, and the sacrifices demanded by loyalty. Elena, born into a modest immigrant family, is taught early that her extraordinary beauty is both her greatest gift and her sole value. Driven by her mother's relentless ambition, elena rises from her humble beginnings to the heights of wealth and power as the wife of a billionaire, yet she cannot escape the shadow of familial expectations and exploitation.

Through vivid characters and elegant prose, tony cointreau explores themes of resilience, betrayal and unflagging friendship. A tragedy of riches is a poignant meditation on the cost of loyalty, the allure of power, and one woman's quest to define her worth beyond what others demand of her.

A TRAGEDY of RICHES

A NOVEL

Also by Tony Cointreau

Ethel Merman, Mother Teresa...and Me
A Memoir
My Improbable Journey from Châteaux in France
to the Slums of Calcutta

A Gift of Love:
Lessons Learned from My Work and Friendship
with Mother Teresa

A TRAGEDY
of RICHES

A NOVEL BY

TONY COINTREAU

Winsor Publications
New York, NY 10021
www.TonyCointreau.com

With affection and gratitude to Sharon Nettles, an outstanding editor and a good friend.

With appreciation to Leah Abrahams of Mixed Media Memoirs, LLC, for guidance and support in this project.

Cover and interior design by Jason Davis.

Publisher's Cataloging-in-Publication Data

Names: Cointreau, Tony, author.
Title: A tragedy of riches : a novel / Tony Cointreau.
Description: New York, NY: Winsor Publications, 2025.
Subjects: LCSH Rich people--Fiction. | Family--Fiction. | Marriage-
-Fiction. | Immigrants--Fiction. | BISAC FICTION / General
Classification: LCC PS3603.O56 T73 2025 | DDC 813.6--dc23

Hardcover ISBN: 979-8-9928408-0-3
Softcover ISBN: 979-8-9928408-1-0
eBook ISBN: 979-8-9928408-2-7

Manufactured in the United States of America

To my beloved Rosie
with all my love forever

Everything I have written is true.
Only the names have been changed
to protect the guilty.

～

PROLOGUE

Guards checked everyone's identification before allowing the limousines to pass through the gates of the historic mansion.

Philip Zimmerman glanced at his beautiful wife, Elena, who was sitting next to him in their limousine. After more than a decade of marriage, he still marveled at her perfect oval face, her rich auburn hair, her high cheekbones and deep-set dark brown eyes. He also approved of what she was wearing: a pale cream-colored beaded evening gown she had bought at Givenchy in Paris a few months before, and the diamond drop earrings and a diamond bracelet he had bought for her at Van Cleef & Arpels. She had left the matching necklace at home; it would have competed with the beaded bodice of her gown.

She had chosen her jewels well for tonight, he thought. It could have been a difficult decision, with so many to pick from, including full sets of diamonds and sapphires, diamonds and rubies, diamonds and emeralds, and plain diamonds—all with stones the size of a pigeon's egg.

Elena looked at her left hand, where, on the fourth finger, next to her wedding ring, she always wore the perfect thirty-carat blue-white diamond from Harry Winston that Philip had given her when they were married. She once confided in a friend that for her the ring was like a permanent symbol of the only thing her family had taught her to believe she had to offer—her beauty. She had even kept that huge diamond ring on her finger when she went diving from their lavish private yacht into the transparent blue waters of Saint-Tropez, where extreme luxury seemed almost commonplace.

Elena was twenty-five years younger than Philip, whom she had married when he was almost sixty. Now that she was nearing forty, not only her husband but also the rest of the world still marveled at her perfect classic features. In the early 1950s, Elena had been widely acclaimed as one of the ten most beautiful women in the world, along with Elizabeth Taylor and Ava Gardner. It was not an exaggeration, and over the ensuing years she had lost none of the beauty and charisma that fascinated every man she had met since the day she was born into a modest Italian family in upstate New York.

She knew only too well what was in store for her this evening, but she held her head high and stared at the back of the chauffeur's head with more or less the same poise and dread as Marie Antoinette on her way to the guillotine.

Once the guests were inside the mansion, flashbulbs popped as private inner circle photographers captured another moment in history—a moment when a grateful host paid homage to the small army of business moguls who had been influential in placing him in one of the most powerful positions in the world. Gratitude may not have been a word widely used in those circles, but other men's usefulness and power were certainly acknowledged and had to be catered to.

The host and hostess greeted the Zimmermans as politely and graciously as was expected, the host showing only a momentary pause in his carefully professional demeanor the moment he laid eyes on the lovely Elena.

Elena had attended many other important functions at the mansion, and invariably found herself in an uncomfortably intimate position, with her host's hardness pressing against her on the dance floor, or his too familiar hand groping under the table like an infatuated schoolboy while she sat at a place of honor next to him at dinner.

If he imagined her to be just another conquest, unable to resist the aura of his enormous power, he had not taken into account the woman herself. He did not yet know that this woman he was attempting to seduce—with both of their spouses in the same crowded room—had a rare quality. She had no fear of man or of death, which strangely turned out to be one of her most seductive traits. She was a woman who could not be intimidated, even by one of the most influential men in the world. By now she had already seen it all and was not impressed by power or position. The only thing that mattered to her was one's integrity as a human being.

On this night, although the host's eyes often lingered on Elena's beaded bodice during dinner, he had the good grace to keep his hands above the table. Neither Elena nor the hostess, who was well aware of her husband's proclivities, was lulled into a false sense of security, but Elena's easygoing wit and the aura of glamour that she generated wherever she went, made the many courses of the meal enjoyable for everyone else.

As tradition dictated, after dinner the men and women temporarily went their separate ways—the women for coffee and girl talk and the men for cigars and political maneuvering. As soon as the proper time had elapsed and the sexes were expected to mingle again, the host casually made his way to the antique chair Elena was seated in. This seemingly discreet move was not lost on his wife, who had carefully guarded her position as "the wife" for several decades. She knew that it would be ruinous for her husband to flaunt his infatuations in too public a manner.

However, some good bourbon and the air of danger and excitement that Elena often inspired in the opposite sex could bring out inappropriate behavior in even the most brilliant of men. This evening was no exception. While a band played in a corner of the great room, the host leaned over and asked Elena, "Would you like to dance?"

Having no way to gracefully deny the request, Elena answered, "Yes, of course," and smiled at the many pairs of eyes that stayed riveted on the couple as they walked to the dance floor.

Elena's dance partner gave the appearance of the perfect gentleman as he pressed closer to her and whispered in a husky voice, "You know, my dear, that an assignation for the two of us could easily be set up. I could arrange for your husband to be called into a high-level meeting he could not ignore. Then we could be alone together. I needn't tell you how often I've imagined the many ways your sensual mouth could pleasure me while Philip is otherwise engaged. I promise you won't be disappointed. If you let me feel your beautiful naked body and please me in the ways that I most enjoy, I could make the experience advantageous for both you and Philip."

Anyone who knew the real Elena would have comprehended that this was the wrong tactic. Not that he ever had a chance, with his overbearing, lewd manner. But threats or bribery were abhorrent to Elena, who took a perverse pleasure in facing down any man who tried to intimidate her. It was just no longer possible for a man to do that. She had survived it all. She also knew that Philip was important enough in his own right not to have to seek favors from anyone.

Not wanting to make a scene, and knowing that her hostess was watching their every move, Elena laughed lightly and turned towards an open window to breathe in the fresh night air. Her would-be suitor took advantage of the occasion, and casually put his strong arm around her back and his large hand on her right shoulder. In that instant, with their backs to the other guests, he pushed his warm hand down into her bodice and gripped her breast with his fingers.

Elena had two older brothers, and as a child she was known as a bit of a tomboy whose diminutive figure belied a strong body; she could defend herself better than most. As an adult, she was not at all the fragile belle some people assumed her to be. With the other guests still unaware of their host's appalling behavior, she now used a very effective trick she had learned from her two older brothers years before. She reached up with her right hand until she found the fleshy part of her host's upper right arm, and then she twisted the soft flesh with her thumb and forefinger, using all the considerable strength in her tiny body.

Only the hostess guessed the reason for the sudden cry of pain from the dance floor. She may even have smiled inwardly at the tears her husband wiped from his eyes as he turned back to face the room. Elena herself let out a little cry, a laugh meant to cover up an awkward encounter.

This man, who was not used to being rebuffed by anyone, attempted to regain a modicum of dignity as he strode out of the room, his rage well hidden behind a false smile.

A while later, his wife left the salon to go find her husband. She knocked on the door of the powder room where he was assessing the damage to his upper arm, and called out to him, "Our guests are ready to go home, but they wonder where you have gone to. They don't want to leave the White House without saying 'Goodnight' to their host, the President of the United States."

CHAPTER 1

E lena was strangely silent on the ride home, and
Philip did not quite understand the little smile
that played at the corners of her mouth. She was thinking how far her family had come since the days when
her parents had arrived as immigrants from Italy, with
nothing but her mother's ambition and her father's will-
ingness to work hard.

In the spring of 1915, a sixteen-year-old girl by the
name of Maria Manziano, who would one day be Elena's
mother, had arrived at Immigration in New York City

with her twenty-five-year-old husband, Ernesto, at her side and a six-month-old infant, Carlo, in her arms.

Maria had been eight years old when she lost her mother to tuberculosis, and fourteen when her father had died of blood poisoning after stepping on a rusty nail. Left alone, and determined to have a better life, she had married Ernesto, and after Carlo was born, she convinced him that they should accept her uncle Mauro's invitation to join him in America.

It had been a long, harrowing trip, with the three of them crowded into a tiny windowless cabin located somewhere in the bowels of the ship. Their home, on a small farm that had been in Ernesto's family for several generations in a little village outside of Naples, seemed a long way from the dock, where hundreds of bewildered immigrants, most of whom spoke little English, were doing their best to answer the confusing questions thrown at them by harried officials.

Maria was looking for her Uncle Mauro. She was near tears when she spotted Uncle Mauro waving frantically at them from a distance. With one of her tall husband's muscular arms firmly around her and the baby, and his other holding the small cardboard suitcase that held all their worldly belongings, they fought their way through the crowds and into the huge embrace of her beloved uncle.

"Uncle Mauro, it's so good to finally be here," she said to the slight, balding older gentleman, who took out his handkerchief to dry her tears.

Ernesto helped load his wife and child into Uncle Mauro's rickety Model T Ford. The bumpy ride to Watkins Glen, New York, felt like pure luxury after the confines of the ship.

There was so much to say, and yet Maria spoke little. The shock of finally having made this trip and facing a new life was both frightening and exhilarating at the same time. Her main concern now was for their baby, Carlo, sleeping peacefully in her arms.

Uncle Mauro's wife, Francesca, was awaiting their arrival. "Welcome, children. Come in. There's not much room in our apartment, but then again, we're all used to making do with very little. I made some soup and pasta for us. It's the best I could do with so many mouths to feed. At least Maria can take care of the baby's needs. Come in."

As they entered her small, comfortably furnished living room, Francesca screwed up her nose, crossed herself, and said, "Dear Mother of God, you both need to change your clothes and bathe immediately. Weren't you able to wash on the boat? Phew! We can't have that smell in our house. I hope that the little one is clean, at least."

"Oh, yes, Aunt Francesca," Maria replied, "he is, but there was only enough water for us to bathe him. I'm sorry, dear Aunt, but I'm afraid that Ernesto and I need to bathe and wash all our clothes as soon as possible."

"Well, it can't be too soon for me! In the meantime, Mauro can lend you something to wear until your things are dry. Mauro, you hold the baby until they've finished cleaning up. Oh dear, I hope we can get that smell out of the house. It's making me ill. I'm not a well woman, you know!"

"I'm sorry, Aunt Francesca, but we did the best we could—"

Before Maria could finish her sentence, Francesca had rushed to her bedroom with a handkerchief covering half her face.

It was clear to Ernesto that they could not live with his wife's relatives for very long. When he and Maria had retired to their tiny room, he said, "Your aunt is not an easy woman to deal with. Back home in Italy, she had the reputation of finding fault in everyone and everything. I know sometimes she would pretend to play the role of generous hostess, but behind her guests' backs she was ruthless with her criticism. Uncle Mauro must love you very much to have talked her into letting us stay with them."

Ernesto had been a part-time barber in Italy and was quite good at it. The next day he went out looking for work, and came home in a jubilant mood. "Maria, I've just been to the local barbershop down the street, and guess what? The owner can use some help, and he gave me a job—full time. Isn't it wonderful?"

"Congratulations! But you're not the only one with news. Aunt Francesca asked me if I would like to help her embroider napkins and tablecloths for a local store to sell. I can do it at home and take care of the baby as well. If nothing else, it will pay for our room and board while we are under their roof."

A few weeks later Ernesto came home from work and announced, "Maria, I have more good news today. Now that I have a steady job, we can afford the apartment that's for rent above the bar down the block. You can be the mistress of your own home, and you will no longer have to listen to your Aunt Francesca's daily list of complaints."

Maria knew her aunt well enough to understand that the moment they moved into their new apartment, Francesca would try to poison everyone's mind against the "ingrates" she had taken into her home "out of the goodness of her heart"—even though she had never paid Maria so much as a penny for her embroidery.

"I'm sorry that Uncle Mauro will be subjected to Aunt Francesca's constant criticisms and harangues about us," Maria said to Ernesto, "but he's an adult and he knew what she was like before he married her—he knew how difficult and impossible she can be."

Francesca was one of the largest women in town, short and fat with red splotches all over her face. It did not help matters that the fatter and uglier she became, the more she resented her younger, prettier, and thinner niece, who had a sylphlike figure, luxuriant dark hair, brown almond-shaped eyes, and perfect skin. Although she was still a teenager, Maria had never had so much as a blemish on her face.

Maria was wise enough to know that the only way to deal with her aunt was to say nothing and to stay as far away from the woman as possible.

—

The next year Maria gave birth to another child, a handsome baby boy they named Angelo—their little "angel."

She doted on her two babies and often took them with her to Ernesto's barbershop, which he—"the best and only employee"—had purchased when the elderly owner retired.

To Maria, the obvious next step was for Ernesto to set up a space in which she could have a beauty parlor. He agreed, and built rooms that also provided storage and a nursery for the children. Of course he built a separate entrance so the ladies could not only have their hair done but also gossip in private. Maria soon found that she was as gifted as her husband at this kind of work, and all her clients told her that she had golden hands.

Francesca, however, went around town saying, "The whole idea is ridiculous. A decent mother should keep her babies at home where they belong."

Maria told Ernesto, "It is just as well that Aunt Francesca never comes into the shop, because her hair would be impossible to do anything with. There would be no way to please her. The only thing she would enjoy would be having a larger audience to gossip with and complain to."

Inexplicably, business in the beauty shop began to decline.

Eventually Maria found out that her aunt had been going around town saying, "You know, our Maria is a lovely girl, but some of her clients are losing their hair and others are picking up lice from having their hair done in the shop."

After Maria got word of the scandalous news her aunt was spreading, she began plotting her own plan of attack. No grass had ever grown under Maria's feet. She was clever and had found a way out of her village in Italy and all the way to America at the age of sixteen. If this teenager could manipulate Ernesto, who was considerably older, then she should have no trouble stopping her drunken aunt from spreading vicious rumors that could destroy her hairdressing business. Francesca would soon learn that her niece was not one to fool with.

When Maria and her husband had been living in her aunt and uncle's home, she had learned that the moment Uncle Mauro went off to work in the morning, Aunt Francesca would start drinking Fernet Branca. She always said, "It's necessary for my digestion."

However, there was quite a strong alcoholic content in this "medicinal" liquor, which tasted bitter and kept her in a happy state of intoxication. Needless to say, her character and her language did not improve as the day went on. Francesca also prided herself on being a pillar of the Catholic Church despite her foul mouth, though she never took the time to think that those two things didn't go very well together.

Every day around noon Francesca had insisted that her niece take the babies to the neighborhood park for at least an hour. She would tell Maria, "The fresh air will be good for the bambinos."

The young mother was only too happy to get out of the negative atmosphere of the house and take a break from her endless hours of embroidery while Francesca nipped at her drinks.

One day, when the weather was turning cold, she had returned from the park early because she feared that Carlo was getting the sniffles. And that's when she was greeted by the sight of her naked aunt doing something with the rotund and equally naked butcher that, in her innocence, she thought only dogs and farm animals did. The two lovers were so engrossed in their sexual escapades that they never saw Maria, who quickly and quietly backed out of the room.

Maria had soon discovered that the butcher, whose store was under her uncle's apartment, would close his shop for an hour in the middle of the day and climb up the back stairs, where Francesca would be waiting with a bottle of wine and an open robe. The butcher was only slightly uglier and fatter than his midday lover, but he had an amazing endowment that enormously pleased his already half-drunk upstairs neighbor, who was ready to delight him with any part of her body he wished.

A few days later, while Maria had been putting away the laundry, she came across letters in her aunt's lingerie drawer—letters that had passed between Francesca and the butcher, detailing the ways that they could satisfy even more of their sexual natures. They were both insatiable and inventive, and loved to write about their sexual fantasies.

Although Maria was young and seemingly naive, she knew that the unusual sexual content of her aunt's incriminating letters might someday be of use to her. It was only too simple to take them from Francesca's dresser drawer and slip them into the pocket of her apron while

Francesca was taking a nap after a morning of nipping at the Fernet Branca.

And now Francesca was jeopardizing Maria's business. One morning, after Ernesto had gone to work, Maria left her children with a neighbor and walked over to her uncle's house for a visit with her aunt. Francesca had no choice but to invite her in. Maria declined the obligatory offer of a cup of coffee and got right to the point. "I hear that you have been saying bad things about my shop and my work to the other ladies in town."

The aunt attempted to feign surprise and denied everything. "It's those awful, jealous women who are telling you these lies. They hate me because I have the nicest home and the most handsome and successful husband in the neighborhood. Terrible, terrible women! How could they be so cruel, especially when they all know how fragile my health is?"

Maria took a deep breath and controlled herself. Although the subject of her aunt's ill health came up regularly, it was never quite clear to anyone, not even Uncle Mauro, exactly what the problem was. In spite of drinking so much Fernet Branca, Francesca seemed as hearty as a bull. Maria guessed that the "ill health" was just a ploy to gain sympathy and attention and to excuse her often drunken and cruel behavior.

"Let me make something perfectly clear, dear aunt. I know all about you and your lunchtime lover downstairs. I have seen it with my own eyes. And if anyone should doubt me, may I ask if you have checked your lingerie drawer lately?"

Everything on Francesca's face, including the purple blotches, turned pale. She was shocked to discover the ruthlessness that lay beneath Maria's always-sweet demeanor. She had not checked the lingerie drawer in quite some time, but she was perfectly aware of what Maria probably had in her hands. However, she was not giving up so easily.

"You little ingrate. I take you, your dullard of a husband, and your sniveling child into my home. I feed you, give you a warm bed to sleep in, and this is the way I get repaid. I'm not a well woman, as you know, and the strain of your ungratefulness might well be the end of me."

With that she collapsed on the couch in a river of howls and tears.

"Aunt, we were very grateful for your generosity when we arrived. But I think Ernesto has paid you back any cost our stay might have incurred. I also did your embroidery work for the store while we were here and you never paid me a penny for any of it. So I don't believe we owe you anything further.

"Now, as to your stories about my shop, tomorrow you will come and ask me to do your hair. You will make a big fuss about the wonderful job that I did. You will also retract all the ugly things you said to the women in town about my work and come in once a week to have your hair done—with a smile on your face.

"If you do not do everything I say, your letters will find their way to the parish priest, Father Giacomo, to your repulsive lover's wife, and to anyone of any importance in this town. Make no mistake, dear Aunt Francesca, you will be ruined. I trust that I will see you tomorrow morning for your hair appointment at ten o'clock sharp. Good day."

Maria made her own way out the door, leaving a stunned Francesca alone on the couch.

CHAPTER 2

By 1919 the Manziano family, after only four years in America, was doing very well. They had even managed to purchase a small house. But the most life-changing experience for them that year was the birth of their third child, a beautiful baby girl they called Elena.

Her parents and brothers doted on her. Maria repeatedly said, "You must treat her gently. God has made her so beautiful because she's special. My Elena will go far in life with the gifts that God has given her."

It was evident from the day the exceptionally beautiful baby was born that Maria had a steely determination in her expectations for Elena's future—the same determination that had made her latch on to Ernesto when her father died, that had brought them to America, and that had saved her new business from Aunt Francesca's evil tongue. So far her strength had helped her to accomplish a great deal, but the ambitions she harbored for her daughter went far beyond the norm.

Her sons were good looking but had no special gifts that she could put in the bank; Angelo was a jokester and Carlo the studious one. Although Maria loved them both, she knew the advantage that great beauty could give a woman, and pinned all her hopes for her family's future on this glorious little girl.

By the time Elena was five, when she would sit on the porch of her family home in a rocking chair Ernesto had built, people who passed by the house would stop and come up to the porch where the child sat with an air of grace, and exclaim how beautiful she was. If they reached out to touch a part of the magic they saw in this extraordinary creature, the little girl would say, with no particular affectation, "Don't touch me, I'm pretty." It was not said out of vanity; it was simply what she had been told from the day she was born.

But Elena was so much more than just a beautiful child. What few people saw was the love and compassion that had also been born within her: she had a heart that could embrace everyone in the world. Her intelligence surprised her elders with its perception, and her deep-set brown eyes looked through one with a wisdom beyond her years. Ultimately, though, her family raised her to believe that her only asset was her beauty.

When it came to her brothers, who loved to laugh and play in the rough-and-tumble world that young boys enjoy so much, Elena was right there with the best of them. Her ability to share in the fearless—even daredevil—pranks that prepubescent males engaged in, only increased Carlo and Angelo's admiration for their little sister.

Ernesto was completely besotted with his children, Elena in particular, and sometimes would stand in the doorway of her room to admire her while she lay sleeping at night, her silken hair highlighted by moonlight.

As for Maria, she fervently believed that Elena was her ticket out of an unfulfilling life in a small town. She thought they would be better off in New York or Los Angeles, and her beautiful daughter was the one who was destined to make her dreams a reality, regardless of the price Elena might pay. Maria had a remarkable ability to turn a blind eye to anything she didn't want to see, and nothing mattered to her but the future she wanted for her daughter—and therefore for herself and the rest of her family.

Elena, being an unusually astute child, was well aware of her mother's obsessive ambition. She resented the burden it placed on her at too early an age, but at the same time she could see that because of it, she was the only person in the world who could stand up to her overpowering and manipulative mother.

Early on, Elena also understood that something about her mere physical presence brought not only boys but also grown men to their knees. She instinctively knew that her brothers were budding men and therefore not immune to her already developing feminine wiles, although the boys were still too young to understand the sexual implications of her charms. But to Elena, her extraordinary beauty was the true source of her power over them all—the only power she felt she had in the world.

CHAPTER 3

When Elena turned twelve, the womanly beauty that had always been her destiny came into full bloom. She was a good girl, and although she enjoyed the growing attention from the boys in school, her brothers watched her every move. Any boy who came too close was cause for concern. Ernesto had warned them to keep an eye on their sister and step in if anyone made an attempt to flirt with the pride of the Manziano family. The boys did an excellent job, which pleased Elena to a certain extent, since she looked upon her two handsome brothers simply as two more admiring men in her life. She didn't know how to differentiate between appropriate and inappropriate relationships. For her, they were all men. Even Carlo and Angelo had blurred the lines between protecting their baby sister and the jealousy they felt when other boys spoke to her.

—

It was around this time that Ernesto had a phone call from the elderly man who had retired and sold him his barbershop in Watkins Glen, and subsequently moved to Endicott, New York. He said, "A large space has become available here, in the center of town. I think it would be ideal for you. Not only is there more room for a barbershop and Maria's beauty salon, but you can also rent an apartment upstairs that would be just the right size for your family."

The family was thrilled at the opportunity and immediately made arrangements to move to Endicott.

A week before they were to leave, Maria was in the back room of her shop preparing some dye for one of her customers. The dye nearly fell out of her hands when she overheard one of the ladies whispering, "Isn't it sad that the Manzianos have to leave town because their little girl has been fooling around with so many of the local boys? Francesca says that she may even be in a family way. You know how close she is to her husband's niece, so she should know!"

"Oh yes, I heard the same thing. What a shame—and such a pretty girl, too," said another.

It took all of Maria's self-control to go back into the store and finish her customers' hair as if nothing had happened. She had survived worse than that in her life, and had dealt with each situation in a most efficacious manner.

The day before their departure, Maria took Aunt Francesca's damning letters from their hiding place and sent anonymous copies to everyone in town who mattered, along with a note about the vicious stories being spread about an innocent child.

Before they left Watkins Glen, Maria told her whole family of Aunt Francesca's actions and how she had taken care of the situation. She knew that rumors would spread and she preferred telling them the truth in her own words. The thought of Elena's leaving town under a cloud of insinuation and lies was more than any of them could bear. The boys knew that they would miss their Uncle Mauro, who often took them on hikes in the woods or fishing by the side of the stream close to his house; but they felt that they could never forgive his wife for her evil tongue.

Maria was gratified to hear that Father Giacomo based his next sermon on the sin of spreading malicious rumors. What only the good priest and Aunt Francesca knew was that he refused to give her absolution for her sins until she told him the whole truth about her affair with the butcher and her lies about Elena. The ladies who were in the church on the day Francesca went to confession were self-righteously amused at the inordinate amount of time the woman with the evil tongue had to spend at the altar saying prayers as the penance given to her by the priest.

—

The Manzianos' new home in Endicott was a dream come true, especially after all the emotions surrounding the move. They were having Sunday dinner in their new home on a beautiful spring day when the doorbell rang. As usual, the boys fell all over each other racing to be the first one to answer the door. Angelo, who had managed to trip his less-coordinated brother, got there first and froze at the sight that greeted him. There, on the other side of the doorway, stood Aunt Francesca, with tears streaming down her face and a damp hankie clutched in her hand.

The gaudy makeup was gone and her clothes were wrinkled and dirty. For the first time the boys saw a real flesh-and-blood woman, not the false and pretentious aunt they had always known.

In a moment everyone crowded around the doorway to see why the two lively boys were suddenly speechless. Ernesto looked as though he wanted to hit the woman, but Maria took charge and spoke with a deadly quiet tone to her voice.

"Get away from my house. What are you doing here, anyway? Haven't you done enough damage to our family?"

The boys were about to slam the door in her face when Elena pushed everyone aside, stepped forward, and drew her aunt into the house. Elena then surprised everyone by gently taking the weeping woman in her arms and consoling her as though Aunt Francesca were the child.

The family was too shocked to react to the young girl's show of kindness. It was a real Christlike moment that none of them would ever forget.

Elena sat her aunt down in a cozy armchair and held her hand until she was calm enough to speak. At first it was not easy to understand her, but she became more coherent after Elena put a cup of hot tea in her hands.

It turned out that after the scandal broke, she had been ostracized by almost everyone in town. Then Mauro, to whom she had been married for twenty years, had told her, "You're an evil woman. Please leave this house. I never want to lay eyes on you again."

Her tears kept on flowing as she looked around helplessly and asked, "What have I done? Now I have nothing, and not even my own husband wants me. I know I'm a silly old woman, but I wanted so much out of life and was never able to find it. I see a beautiful young girl like Elena and I could scream at the horror of my wasted life. I was not given her gift of great beauty or wit. I'm doomed to the life of a penniless, lonely old woman that nobody wants.

"I don't know why I came here today. You should be the last people in the world who would want to see my ugly face but I have nowhere to go. I am so alone and that is the worst thing in the world—to be alone."

The tears were now coming down Elena's cheeks as well, but she let them flow. Her aunt was a human being after all. Imperfect—but a real breathing human being, in pain. And Elena believed that no one should be crucified for that.

It was undoubtedly Elena's compassion and innocence that moved her parents to offer rest and comfort to this beaten woman who had appeared on their doorstep and asked for their forgiveness. That day Elena taught her family the real meaning of love in action.

～

After an exhausted Aunt Francesca was put to bed in one of the boys' rooms, the family sat down to discuss what to do with the problem that had just walked into their home.

The pragmatic Maria said, "To keep her here indefinitely would be impossible. First of all, we don't have enough room for another adult in the house, and secondly, the chances are that once she feels secure again she will still be a difficult woman to live with."

Elena went to her father and asked, "Papa, why don't you speak to Uncle Mauro and tell him what happened today and how Aunt Francesca was truly heartbroken at losing him? Surely he must have cared for her once. Twenty years is a long time to love someone. Maybe he's too proud to make amends for something he may have said in a moment of anger. Please Papa, do it for me. Do it for Aunt Francesca. Do it for all of us."

A few days later, Uncle Mauro arrived in Endicott and spent the afternoon by the side of a brook with his wife. They talked, they laughed, and they cried. The woman who returned to the Manzianos' house was no longer the pathetic creature who had arrived on their doorstep the Sunday before. She was holding her husband's hand and smiling shyly like a schoolgirl. That evening the two of them went back to their home in Watkins Glen, with hope for a new beginning.

After they had left, Maria hugged her daughter tightly and prayed that the miracle she had manifested because of her love would continue throughout her life.

CHAPTER 4

E ducation was a top priority for Maria. It had been
a luxury she could ill afford for herself, but it was a
necessity for her children if they were to achieve her ambitions. She knew that Elena would have a better chance
of finding a rich and successful Prince Charming if she
left the small town of Endicott for a sophisticated college elsewhere.

To some degree, Ernesto shared Maria's ambition
for their children; he always told them, "You know how
hard your mother and I have worked ever since you
were born. We have always been happy to do so. Your

mother's dream is to give you the opportunity to be somebody important. We came here because America is a wonderful country where anything is possible. Do what you have to do to make your dreams come true."

Maria went around town crowing, "My oldest, Carlo, plans to go to medical school in Los Angeles and he will be a successful doctor, and my Angelo is going to be a famous movie star.

"Of course you all know my little Elena, who is the most popular girl in her class and makes the best grades. Everyone loves her, even the other girls. She will make us very proud when she finds a rich, successful husband who will shower her with jewels and clothes that show off her beautiful face and figure. She will have her pick of the best men in the world and she will be very happy."

When the time came for Elena to choose a college, she asked her parents if she could go to college in Florida.

"Mama, some of my friends say it's a wonderful place where many rich families send their children. Think of all the new friends I can make."

Naturally, the magic word for Maria was "rich" and plans were made for this clever, top-of-her-class student to move to a world far from anything or anyone she had ever known. For the first time in her life she would be away from the watchful eye of her parents and her sometimes overbearing brothers.

~

The moment she arrived in Florida, Elena felt as though her life had just begun. It was as though she had been marking time during her first eighteen years. Other students were homesick and crying at night, but Elena felt a freedom she had never known before. She wanted to shake them and say, "Let's all get a car and go somewhere!"

Once the young men got a look at the new girl on campus, much of their homesickness went out the window while testosterone took over their emotions. Both men and women were drawn to her; she had that indefinable thing called "it," or glamour, combined with an air of mystery and abandon. Wherever she went there was fun. Although she had been born with a talent for flirting, she did not yet need the validation of physical love. At this point in her life the attention she received from the boys was simply a lovely, fun game—

until she met the one boy who would change her life forever.

—

"Hi, my name's Bruce Osborne. I've seen you around campus for the last week and I wanted to meet you. It's kind of hard, though, with all the other guys flocking around."

Bruce was a tall, handsome, blond boy whose sparkling blue eyes immediately attracted Elena. She had already noticed him around school and had been told by some of the other girls that he was a promising athletic star who came from an important family in Kansas.

Her deep-set brown eyes were almost misty when she spoke. "I'm Elena, and I'm happy to meet you, Bruce."

"My mother is here to help me get settled in, or I would ask you to dinner tonight. Maybe we could do it over the weekend?"

"We can have dinner anytime. I'd love it." And she meant it with all her heart. She thought he was the most beautiful man she had ever seen—and those eyes! She prayed his mother would not be staying for too long.

The weekend came and went but she never heard from Bruce, the first boy in her life who she prayed would call. One Sunday evening Elena was sitting in a little café with some friends when she spotted Bruce at another table with an attractive older woman who she supposed was his mother.

As soon as he saw Elena he excused himself and came over to say, "I'm so sorry about our dinner but my mother decided to stay on for a few more days and I couldn't leave her on her own. I hope you understand. Let's make a date as soon as she leaves. By the way, would you like to meet her?"

"Of course, I'd be happy to meet your mother. She must love you very much to come and help you get settled in college. Come on. Let's go say hello. She may think we're rude if we let her sit by herself while we talk."

Elena had been born with a sixth sense and an intuition she did not yet understand, and when she walked over to the older woman, she felt a sudden shiver like ice run down her spine, but she was so taken with Bruce that she ignored it. At the table she saw a beautifully dressed and obviously wealthy woman who tried desperately to look younger than her years. The girl could see the remnants of a once-beautiful woman, but time had not been kind, no matter how heavy the makeup or how blonde the hair.

"This is my mother, Kay. Kay, this is Elena, the girl I was telling you about."

"Of course. You're even more beautiful than I expected. My dear, you must be very careful of all the men who will be seduced by your beauty. It can be a dangerous game for someone as young and innocent as you. It's lovely to have met you. Now Bruce, darling, you must sit back down and finish your dinner before it gets cold."

As she walked back to her other friends, Elena felt the dismissal in Kay Osborne's voice. She didn't quite understand why, but she knew that Bruce's mother was a force to be reckoned with and someone she did not really care to meet again. She hoped that the older woman would soon go back to Kansas.

As the months went by, every time Elena and Bruce made a date to go out together, it seemed that Kay was on her way in or out of Florida. She always had an excuse to visit with her darling Bruce just when Elena felt they might be making some headway in their budding relationship. Finally, Elena could take it no more and managed to be busy with other social engagements whenever Bruce called her. Sometimes she would run into Bruce and Kay in a club or on campus. Everyone was polite, but Elena never lingered. She couldn't bear

Mrs. Osborne's cold demeanor or the bewildered puppy dog look on Bruce's face each time they met.

⁓

The college years flew by, and each year Maria would quiz her daughter about the potential husbands she had met. She cared little about Elena's scholastic accomplishments. The only grades she was concerned about were Carlo's, as he would soon be entering medical school in California.

Just before graduation, Elena ran into Bruce at a party given by a mutual friend. In actuality, Bruce had asked this friend to invite Elena but made him promise not to tell her that he was coming.

On the night of the party, Kay was out of town. She had relaxed her guard and her trips to Florida had become less frequent after she found out that Elena had decided to stop seeing Bruce.

Bruce was one of the first to arrive at the party. He wanted to be there when Elena came in, so he could talk to her before any of the other seniors moved in on her. She was the only girl he had wanted to be with for the four years he had spent in college. His only fear was that he had waited too long to make his feelings known, and now it might be too late. He had no idea that Elena had also lain awake nights fantasizing about being alone with Bruce and wishing that his mother would disappear.

"Elena!"

It took her a moment to regain her composure. She said in as casual a manner as possible, "Bruce, what a surprise! How nice to see you here."

The words "Where is your mother?" were left unsaid, although they were on the tip of her tongue.

"I wonder if we could go somewhere quiet, just the two of us, and talk? I have something to ask you."

"Sure, I'd love to go somewhere quiet with you, Bruce. You don't know how uncomfortable I am at these noisy gatherings. I don't even drink, which makes it worse."

"Come on, Elena, I know just the place. If you don't mind, the quietest place I know is my apartment, and since I live alone, no one will disturb us. I promise it's okay. I'll be a perfect gentleman. I only want to talk. I've wanted to for so long. Please, come with me for just a while."

"Okay, but let's not leave together or people will talk. I'll meet you down the street in ten minutes."

They were both silent during the walk to his apartment. Neither of them wanted to open the floodgates of their emotions until they were safely inside.

The two youngsters talked for hours. Once they started there was no stopping them. Love was the order of the day and they were in love. They had always been in love.

Elena was too naive to question Bruce's relationship with the mother he referred to as "Kay." Kay Osborne was not with them that night, and for one perfect evening could not take away the happiness they both felt would live on forever.

The lovers kissed, and although they held hands and melted into each other's aura, they insisted that the purity of their love remain sacred until they had said their marriage vows.

⁓

The day of the wedding was beautiful, a perfect June day. At breakfast, Kay talked nonstop. "Elena, my dear, you look pale. A little rouge would do wonders for your cheeks. I have just the thing. I'll show you later. And maybe we can still do something about that hair. Oh, it's a perfectly lovely color but I think we'd better let my hairdresser put it up for you, so it will show off my antique veil a little more. Oh well, we'll attend to all of that in time for the ceremony. Go on, dear, you're not eating a thing. No wonder you're so thin. Oh, what a heavenly day."

Elena sat quietly, taking it all in, wondering what the day would bring. She knew how to handle her own overbearing mother, who would not be attending the wedding but didn't mind as long as her daughter was marrying into a wealthy family, but Elena wasn't sure what to do about Kay—she didn't want to offend her future mother-in-law, or damage her relationship with her soon-to-be husband.

⁓

The ceremony was held on the immense, tree-lined lawn in front of Kay Osborne's house, which she had built to resemble Tara in Gone With The Wind.

When the day was over and all the guests had departed, Elena went to the elegant rooms that had been assigned as the bridal suite. The rest of the house was tastefully decorated with Chippendale, Queen Anne, and George III antiques, but this little suite was in a different style. The furniture was ornately carved Louis XV, with soft bluish tones, very light and feminine. The walls were covered in pale blue silk, and the ceiling had been painted to look like the sky, with soft clouds passing by. The double bed was covered with embroidered white satin sheets and white lace decorative pillows. The Aubusson carpet echoed the soft colors in the room. Elena thought it was almost too delicate to walk on.

Elena didn't know how long it would be until her new husband would appear, so she took a quick bubble bath, dressed in the silk lace gown and pegnoir that had been laid out on the bed, and brushed out her beautiful thick hair. She wanted everything to be perfect for the first night she would spend with her beloved. She had saved herself for this moment for years, and was trembling with anticipation.

Elena waited. And waited. And waited. As the hours passed, she became increasingly anxious. Finally, at the stroke of midnight, Bruce finally entered the room with a sheepish look on his face.

"Elena, darling, it's been the most beautiful day of my life.…"

They finally fell asleep at dawn, cradled in each other's arms. They stayed that way until they could no longer ignore the persistent knocking on the door.

"Darling, it's Kay. Are you two sleepyheads going to stay in bed all day? It's time for breakfast and we have a full schedule planned for this morning."

"We'll be right there, Kay. Why don't you start without us? We're a little late getting up this morning," Bruce said.

"Bruce, why don't you run down and keep Kay company? I'm awfully tired. Do you think you could make my excuses for missing breakfast? Just say I have a headache or something—anything. I just can't pull myself together as quickly as you and I'd love to luxuriate for a while in the memory of a wonderful night with the most wonderful man in the world. Please, my love, do it for me. I'll be waiting for you when you return."

"All right, my sweet, I'll see that someone brings you something to eat and some tea to start your—excuse me—I mean our—day."

After Bruce had rushed out, Elena felt a loneliness she had never known before, so she decided to brush her lustrous hair, throw on a simple day dress, and surprise Bruce and Kay in the dining room.

As she walked down the stairs and through the massive entryway, she heard voices and stopped in front of the library door. She recognized the voices as those of Bruce and Kay. It sounded like a serious discussion. She moved closer and stood frozen as the words became clear.

"Bruce darling, you will sleep with the girl only when I tell you, and that's final."

"But Mother…"

"Haven't I made it clear to you that my name is KAY, KAY, KAY!!! Not 'Mother!' Say it!"

"Kay," answered a sheepish sounding Bruce.

"You may have a child with the girl—if you must. I suppose it would be nice for you to have an heir. She is pretty so I suppose that you could have done worse. The two of you should be able to make a beautiful child."

Elena's knees became weak, as Kay went on, "Oh, darling, don't you know that Kay knows best? I've always done the right thing by you and someday all your father's fortune will be passed on to you. I want that more than anything. And I want you to know that no one in the universe will ever love you as much as I do. Look at all I've given up for you. I could have married again many times over. But no, I wouldn't share my attention and affection with anyone else. I've worked to build your father's fortune into something very important and made sure that you will have the top position in his company. As I've so often told you, I'll see that you have only the very best. Now, have I made myself clear? You will sleep with that girl only when Kay tells you to. The other nights you will spend with Kay, just like before. I am still a vibrant woman and I would walk through fire for you. Do you understand, my darling?"

"Yes, Kay. I understand."

"Now come and give Kay a big kiss the way you used to before that girl came into our lives."

With those last words Elena crashed to the floor in a dead faint. It was too much to bear.

Kay and Bruce heard Elena hit the floor outside the door and came running.

"I thought you said she was still in bed."

"She was when I left, but she must have changed her mind."

"Oh well, never mind, she might as well know her place sooner rather than later."

When Elena regained consciousness, she was lying on her bed with an anxious Bruce rubbing her hands.

"Oh darling, you had me so worried. What happened to you? I thought you were going to stay in bed. One of the maids was preparing a tray for you. Kay ordered your breakfast herself."

Elena raised herself up on one elbow and tried to get her feet on the floor. She felt as though she was stuck in the middle of a nightmare. Much of what she had heard outside the library door was still too much information for her to absorb, but the general meaning of the conversation was quite clear.

Bruce tried to ease her back on the bed but she fought him off. Kay was nowhere to be seen.

"I heard, Bruce, I heard. Do you understand? You and that woman. She's a monster, Bruce, and she's made you one too. But you'll never see it, will you? She won't let you see it. How long, Bruce? How long has she owned you body and soul?… My God, you probably have no idea."

"Please, darling, it's not the way you think. It's, well, different. When I was a little boy and rebelled against her wishes she told me that if I didn't do as she said, she would die and I would never see her again. It frightened me so. She was all I had. After Daddy died, I would have been all alone if she had died too. I couldn't let that happen. And I was scared—so scared all the time."

Bruce's tears fell on Elena's face, but she hardly felt them. She just knew that she was in a situation she could not accept. Now she had to face the fact that her marriage to Bruce was nothing more than a sham. But she was a highly intelligent young woman and should have known long ago that there was no way out for Bruce as long as Kay held all the deep emotional cards in her hands. Elena could see no alternative for herself but to pack her few belongings and leave while she still had a semblance of sanity left. She feared that if she waited so much as one day she might become one of them. And that would surely be the end of her.

A familiar voice from the doorway suddenly cut through her like a knife. "Bruce, go to my room immediately and stay there until I call for you. I want to be alone with Elena for a while. She needs another woman to talk to. There's nothing you can do for now, darling. Go, dry your tears. Kay will make everything all right."

Elena wished she could put her hands over her ears. She never wanted to hear that voice again. But she knew she had to face her mother-in-law now and end this misery as quickly as possible.

"No, Mrs. Osborne, I have no need to speak to you alone. Bruce might as well hear this now because it would be too painful to have to say it twice."

Elena continued, "I had no intention of hearing your conversation in the library this morning, but I was on my way to join you in the dining room when I heard your voices. I didn't even have to put my ear to the door to clearly hear what has been going on between a mother and her son for longer than I care to think. I may have gone through a ceremony with my husband but he clearly belongs to you—and always will. I'm leaving today, Bruce, and I will never see you again. And if last night we made a child, that child will be mine alone, and I will see to it that neither of you ever has any contact with it."

Kay understood immediately that there was nothing she could say to change Elena's mind. In any case, Kay felt confident that she could eventually make Bruce understand that the marriage had been a big mistake, and that the most important thing was that they still had each other. Kay put her arms around her son and led him back to her room, where she could comfort him in private until she was sure the girl had left for good.

⌒

In later years Elena never knew where she had acquired the strength to leave that house the way she did. On the train back home, Elena had no more tears left to shed. These people had left her feeling numb. But the one thing she knew she still had was her beauty. She had certainly heard it enough all her life to believe it. She decided if that was all she had, then that was what she would use to conquer the male species. If they wanted to enjoy her physical attributes they would have to earn it. This was a game she finally felt ready to play. She was even looking forward to using it as a kind of revenge and a way to prove that her exquisite beauty gave her all the power she needed to make sure that none of them would ever hurt her again.

⌒

Kay quickly arranged for a discreet divorce, and came up with a ready answer for her friends, one that put Elena in the worst possible light.

Maria was naturally devastated at the news of the impending divorce, and Elena never confided in any of her family about the incestuous affair between her husband and his mother at the Osborne mansion. Although Maria ranted and raved to Ernesto about the lost opportunity for her daughter, she hated the thought of how much these people must have hurt her precious child. However, Maria's practical side soon took over and she was confident that another avenue, maybe an even better one, would open up. After all, the girl was barely twenty-two years old.

—

Two months after coming home, Elena asked her mother about certain things that were happening to her body—things she didn't really understand and which frightened her.

Maria wasted no time in taking her daughter to the family doctor, who confirmed what the older woman had instantly suspected. Elena was expecting a child.

When Elena found out, she felt no fear, only a sense of anticipation that one magnificent thing would emerge from the nightmare she had endured during her short marriage.

CHAPTER 5

Maria leaned over Elena's hospital bed and whispered, "Honey, your little girl is as lovely as her mother."

The birth had not been an easy one, but Elena had always had a high threshold for pain and did her part as though she had given birth many times before. This was her moment of victory. For the first time in her life she felt like a real woman and not just a beautiful creature for others to admire.

It was 1941, and most of the world was at war. Angelo, whose acting career had dwindled into obscurity, decided that it would be a good time for him to join the army. Since Elena had always felt a special bond with her brother, she named her little girl Angelina in his honor.

While in the hospital, Elena pondered what to do with the immediate future.

She said to her mother, "Staying in a small town like Endicott is unthinkable, and New York seems too big and impersonal. Maybe Angelina and I could go to Los Angeles, since Carlo is still in medical school there."

Maria immediately agreed. "We are family, so we should make the move together. Ernesto and I will close up the shop, pack up our belongings, and prepare for the trip out west. California will be just the place for us all."

Eventually, Maria and Ernesto found a little house in Burbank, a suburb of Los Angeles, while Elena opted for a small apartment in Hollywood for herself and Angelina.

—

Hollywood was the perfect city for Elena to start a new life. She had a lifelong interest in art, and in the greater Los Angeles area she found the opportunity to see in person some of the works that she had previously seen only in books. She enjoyed visiting art galleries and places such as the Huntington Library and Museum, and began to make her own copies of paintings and sculptures that she loved.

At the same time, the movie studios were in full swing and the town was filled with men looking for another dazzling face to fulfill their fantasies. It was also the day of the "casting couch," when loads of lovely starlets were expected to service the executives with oral sex after work, before it was time for the men to go home to their wives and children.

Elena was smart enough to stay away from that sordid scene and make her own rules. She knew she had a rare beauty, but what she was not aware of was the fascination her independence and charisma also held for every man she met. Soon she had men at her beck and call from morning to night, and she went at it with a vengeance.

Elena had breakfast dates, luncheon dates, dinner dates and even after-dinner dates. She accepted her romantic partners' gifts and lived well on their generosity, but no matter how many men said, "I love you," there were never enough "I love you's" to satisfy the broken and disillusioned young bride that still lived inside her.

She needed all the validation she could get to prove to herself that she was worthwhile, and sex was a part of it. Although she never got any physical pleasure out of the act, she was a good actress and made each man feel that he was the most unforgettable lover in the world. To be on the safe side, she had a small operation to have her tubes tied, ensuring that she would not have to endure an unwanted pregnancy.

When producers spotted her and begged her to at least give motion pictures a chance, she dug her heels in; and to make sure she would not end up like most of the other girls in town, she would shrug her shoulders and say, "All I want is to be a housewife." She had opportunities that most girls in that town would sell their souls to the devil for, and many of them did, but Elena remained firm in her resolve to be in charge of her own destiny.

The one victim in all this turned out to be little Angelina. Her early years were relatively normal, thanks to her grandparents, Maria and Ernesto, who were ready to take charge at a moment's notice. But when she was old enough to go to school, Angelina often walked the streets of Hollywood Boulevard alone after classes, because there was no one at home. Like her mother at that age, she had a strange maturity way beyond her years. In this environment, Angelina became the caretaker and mother, and Elena the untamed daughter, almost as if they had traded places. The one constant in their lives, though, was that both were secure in the knowledge that they adored each other.

~

All in all, Angelina had a most unorthodox upbringing. She was such a bright and sweet child that some of Elena's boyfriends enjoyed playing surrogate father to her, and she often went with her mother on their outings. One of Elena's most loyal admirers, Mack, who was an agent for some of the biggest stars in Hollywood, once took them to the racetrack. That day was a turning point for Elena.

Mack had gone to bet on a horse when a familiar voice behind Elena and Angelina said, "Please don't run away. I just want to say 'Hello' to you, and also to the little girl."

Elena's blood ran cold, but she managed to turn around and say calmly, "Hello, Bruce. Of course you can say hello to Angelina. Angelina, this is Bruce. He's your father."

Angelina was confused. She had never understood why she did not have a daddy like her other friends, and instead of going into his arms she turned away without saying a word.

Bruce was not surprised at the little girl's reaction. It was a lot to spring on a small child. However, he couldn't take his eyes off his daughter. Her dark brown hair and eyes looked so much like her mother. She would never be as stunning as Elena, but she had a presence that belied her years.

Then Bruce said, "Excuse me, Elena, but my mother is here also. I wonder if she could meet her grandchild? I must warn you, though, she's not the same woman you remember. She had some cosmetic surgery a couple of years ago, and, unfortunately, a nerve was cut on one side of her face. Her left cheek has collapsed and half of her mouth has fallen, which makes it hard for her to speak clearly."

Elena looked over to one side and saw a heavily veiled woman with one hand hiding half of her face. She took her child by the hand and led her over to the strange-looking woman and said, "Hello Kay, I'd like you to meet Angelina. Angelina, this is your grandmother, Kay."

The little girl went over to the strange looking woman, and in a tiny voice said, "I have a Nana, but what do I call you?"

The answer was unintelligible, muffled by the hand in front of her face. The little girl put her arms around Kay for just a moment and then ran off to find Mack, who was on his way back from placing his bet.

Elena said a quick goodbye and ran after her little girl, so no one would see the tears in her eyes at the tragedy that had befallen her ex-mother-in-law. Kay looked as proud as ever, but Elena was perceptive enough to see through the woman's bravado. How could she hate this woman after seeing what she had become?

⁓

Shortly after moving to Los Angeles, Elena saw a photo of Philip Zimmerman, a Wall Street giant, in a magazine article, and intuitively told Angelina, "Someday I'm going to marry that man."

Sometime later, in 1949, when one of her boyfriends asked her if a very important friend from New York, Philip Zimmerman, could phone her when he came to town, she remembered her premonition, and said, "Of course."

Elena never tired of saying, "The first time I opened the door for Philip Zimmerman, the man standing in front of me was the same one I had seen in the magazine article, the man I had told Angelina that I would marry one day, and all caution was thrown to the winds."

It didn't hurt that he was rich and from a prominent banking family that controlled much of the world's industry. He was also short and balding, with a prominent nose and thin lips, and about to turn sixty—no one would ever mistake him for Cary Grant. But Elena didn't seem to care about all that. She was desperately drawn to this man.

—

As soon as Maria got wind of her daughter's latest beau, she was in her own pragmatic heaven. "For heaven sake, Elena, marry the man. Do whatever it takes, but marry him!"

This could not have happened at a better time for her family. Maria and Ernesto were finding it hard to start their new business and make ends meet. Angelo had recently married a naive, starstruck girl named Lynn who had fallen hard for the handsome actor—and he had no way to support her. He was out of the army now, and was no longer getting the bit-part acting jobs that had once provided enough money for him to live on; nor did he have any special ambitions that did not involve more talk than anything else. Everyone but Carlo was in a difficult financial situation, and Elena was, as always, their only hope.

CHAPTER 6

P hilip Zimmerman had been born into a prominent Jewish family that had dominated Wall Street and much of the world's industry since the second half of the nineteenth century. In the mid-twentieth century, Jews were still openly discriminated against in New York "society," especially when it came to living in certain apartment buildings on Park or Fifth Avenue. The term that some of these buildings openly used was "restricted," which meant "no Jews allowed"—an ugly premise at best.

One possibly apocryphal story, which was quite popular at the time, was that one of the reigning queens of the cosmetics industry, Helena Rubenstein, had wanted to rent a sumptuous penthouse apartment on Park Avenue. When she was turned down because the building was restricted, she was rich enough to buy the whole building right out from under them, and lived there until she died in her nineties.

Such discrimination had caused no problems for Philip, who had inherited the family townhouse on Fifth Avenue. This mansion was filled with the art that each generation had collected over the years—art that was known throughout the world.

When Philip was born in the last decade of the nineteenth century, the Zimmerman residence was as cold and formal as its inhabitants. The men were expected to wear black tie and the women to dress in formal evening gowns for dinner.

A series of nurses who had been specifically trained for the job were hired to take care of little Philip. They fed him, changed his diapers and saw to all of his needs. They had dinner alone with him until he was old enough to sit with the adults, when he was five or six. Then the nurse, too, dined with the family—not as an equal, but to watch over the child and see that he minded his manners. While at dinner, Philip could answer his elders if he was questioned, but otherwise, children were to be seen and not heard.

Philip's mother had been his father's first wife; after a bitter divorce, she walked out on both her husband and her son. Philip then had a series of self-involved stepmothers. An occasional peck on the cheek was the only human contact they gave him, while his father remained a distant figure who was obeyed by everyone without question.

When Philip was still a toddler, his nurse took him for a play date with one of his friends who lived in a posh apartment building on Fifth Avenue. As they entered the foyer, they saw a woman who looked vaguely familiar to the nurse. The lady silently walked past them and out the front door, and then the nurse suddenly realized who she was—Philip's real mother. The woman had not been capable of acknowledging her own son.

Not knowing how to deal with a child in the house, Philip's father sent him to boarding school at an early age. Unlike many of the other boys, Philip hadn't minded being sent away, since he had always felt like an intruder in the family mansion. His school holidays were much more pleasing when he spent them with friends whose sympathetic parents accepted him into the relative normalcy of their own homes. As for Philip's father, he seemed not to notice the boy's absence. All that mattered was that he had done his duty in seeing that someone was caring for his son and only heir. That was the way children had been dealt with in the Zimmerman family for many generations.

$\sim$

Elena had no idea what she was getting into when she met Philip. She had been raised in a warm Italian family who never wavered in their affection for one another. They could laugh and cry together. A hug or a kiss was not looked upon as something alien to them. No one had to fight for the security that came with the attention it was normal for them to receive from their loved ones.

Philip was not a bad human being; he had just been brought up with no idea of how to relate to another person, or how to have any natural continuity in his emotions. One minute he could make you feel like the dearest person in his life, and the next he would look right through you as if you didn't exist.

When Philip met Elena he was the only one left to run the family business. And he was brilliant at it. That's what he had been bred to do. His personal life, however, was a different matter. He didn't have the emotional stability to stay with a woman for more than a couple of years, and he had already been married five times. He sometimes said that his only regret was that none of his wives had given him a child to carry on the family business.

The one thing that Philip had been taught early in his life was an appreciation of beautiful objects, and the first time he walked into Elena's apartment in Hollywood he was overwhelmed by the beauty that surrounded him. Elena had developed into a talented artist, and had created all the artwork in the four rooms. Her apartment was modest, but she had transformed it into a veritable museum of her own work. Philip, who owned one of the most revered art collections in the world, could not believe the quality of the paintings and sculptures this unique woman had created.

"Elena, is this really your work? It's magnificent."

"Oh, Philip, don't be silly. It's just something I've enjoyed doing since I was a little girl. I've always studied the great artists and their techniques, to learn how they created their masterpieces."

"May I take you out to dinner tonight and talk about it some more? There's so much I'd like to know about you. You know, you're quite a woman of mystery."

Elena simply laughed and said, "I'd love to have dinner with you tonight. Why don't you pick me up at eight o'clock? I promise to be ready on time."

Then she called out, "Oh Angelina, darling, can you leave your homework for a moment? There's a gentleman I'd like you to meet. Philip, this is my daughter Angelina, she's almost nine years old. Angelina, this is Mr. Zimmerman."

"Hello, Angelina," said Philip. He shook her little hand awkwardly and quickly added, "Then I'll see you at eight, my dear."

"Goodbye, Philip," said Elena as she shut the door. She was ecstatic. She took Angelina in her arms and said, "Angelina, that man may not know it yet, but he's going to be your daddy!"

Several dates later, Philip finally did the first impulsive thing in his entire life. He asked Elena to marry him, and she accepted on the spot. He wasn't sure why, maybe it was their mutual appreciation of beautiful things.

As always, Elena was living her life on pure instinct. But she already knew, for better or for worse, Philip was her destiny.

⁓

The next thing on Philip's agenda was to take Elena and Angelina to New York, and proudly show them what their new home looked like. But the moment they walked into the foyer of the townhouse, both mother and daughter froze in horror. It was dark and gloomy, and the first thing they saw was a sixteenth century "prie-dieu," a chair made to kneel on during prayer. Elena thought, This depressing mansion can not possibly be what he considers a home-like atmosphere for us to live in.

Elena and Angelina said little as they toured this mausoleum, and were more than relieved to return to the cheerful suite Philip had reserved for them at the St. Regis Hotel.

Philip knew right away that something was amiss, and he was prepared to do anything to please his prospective bride. He also had the power to change anything she didn't like; he could prove his love and impress her at the same time.

Before he went to the hotel to pick them up for dinner, he called and asked Elena casually, "Darling, which would you prefer, a townhouse or an eighteen-room apartment with six maids' rooms on Park Avenue? I know that you find the old house unlivable and gloomy. We can decorate our new home together, with the finest Impressionist paintings and eighteenth-century furniture we can find."

Elena thought for just a moment and answered, "I think that the apartment would be more pleasant to live in."

For once in his life, Philip was like a schoolboy trying to please his first crush. He had no idea that the trappings of his immense wealth were not the reason that this lovely and talented woman was attracted to him. Yes, Elena had a great sense of aesthetics, but not an ostentatious love of beautiful things. It was one of the enduring qualities that she and Philip shared.

Unlike Elena, Philip had never had the opportunity to feel at home in different levels of society. It was not his fault that he had been born with a platinum spoon in his mouth, and all he had ever known was the rarified world of extreme wealth and luxury. As far as he was concerned, there was little reality to the lives of the less privileged people in the world. He learned a hard lesson the day he took Elena out to see his house on Long Island. Thinking that she would find it amusing, he had the chauffeur stop the car in front of a modest row house along the way.

"Well, what do you think of our country home, darling?"

Elena immediately knew that he thought this would be a hilarious joke, and was deeply offended that he would assume that she might also find humor in it. Elena knew only too well that human beings actually lived in these homes and felt privileged to raise their families there.

"Who do you think I am, Philip? How dare you think that you can make a joke of these people's living conditions just because you were brought up in a golden mansion?"

The rest of the drive to his real home—on the water, with a fifty-foot dock for his yacht, and an Olympic-size swimming pool—was made in silence.

Elena was a woman like no other that Philip had ever met. She bowed down to no one, and had a code of ethics the likes of which he had never seen before.

She was the first woman he had ever known that he felt he could not buy, and the challenge gave him a kind of thrill he had never known before.

CHAPTER 7

It was late in the summer of 1950 when the Manziano family heard the news of Elena's impending marriage. Maria was in her full glory. Nothing she had imagined even came close to this amazing union of her magnificent daughter and the fabulously rich and powerful Philip Zimmerman.

Maria knew that nothing would be more vital to the future of her family than Elena's success in this most important union—a union that could permanently affect all of their lives.

Without hesitation, she and her son Angelo began planning to move from Los Angeles back to Endicott, New York. For the moment, that would be near enough to Elena and her future husband. Angelo and his wife, Lynn, had no choice but to go, since they were living with Maria and Ernesto, and were dependent on them for their food and lodging.

Maria pushed Ernesto night and day to finish their preparations for the move. A week before they were to leave Los Angeles, Ernesto climbed up on a ladder to the second floor, to inspect a shutter that had been making noises during the night. He placed the ladder almost, but not quite, at the right spot, and when he reached over to his right to touch the shutter, he lost his footing and plunged to the ground, sustaining a massive head injury. Within hours he was dead.

Maria was inconsolable—Ernesto had been her life ever since she was a girl. He was the father of her children. She wondered how she could go on without him. Thank God she had Carlo and Angelo at her side.

When Elena heard the news, Philip immediately made arrangements for her to fly to the West Coast and be there for her mother when they buried the only man Maria had ever loved.

No matter what befell her, though, the Widow Manziano was made of steel, and soon after Ernesto's funeral she and Angelo and his wife, Lynn, moved to Endicott without any changes in the schedule. She knew where her priorities lay, and they remained firmly centered on Elena.

The fact that Elena was to marry a tycoon was a dream come true for Maria and her family, who were not at all embarrassed by the prospect of having a free ride in life. They sensed that their chance to grab for the golden ring was finally within their grasp.

⏤

The wedding was a private affair, with Elena and Philip and a justice of the peace. Even Angelina was sent to Endicott to stay with Maria and Angelo and Lynn until the "I do's" had been said.

The groom wore a business suit, and the bride was dressed in a chic black suit and a black hat with a half-veil covering her face. Strangely enough, Philip was in none of the wedding pictures. He insisted that Elena stand alone for the photographer, who only took head shots of the bride. Their wedding pictures ended up looking more like studio portraits of Elena than anything else.

When the ceremony was over, there was no champagne and no reception. Philip took Elena home to their new apartment, which was not yet finished, and then went on to the office, the revered Zimmerman Investments, Inc., where he was king.

While Elena waited alone for Philip that evening, she wondered if she had simply traded Kay Osborne for Zimmerman Investments. When Philip finally arrived, he was met with his wife's full hurt and anger.

"How could you have gone through a marriage ceremony with me this morning and then promptly leave me for Zimmerman Investments? Did you marry me today, or your investment company? The business will be here long after we're gone, but we can never capture the supposedly joyous first moments of our marriage again. Sometimes you can be thoughtful and sweet, but at other times it seems as though ice water runs through your veins. I never know which Philip is going to come through the front door, or who he will be from moment to moment!"

At first, Philip's only concern was that the servants would overhear his wife's anger. He tried his best to assuage her hurt at having been deserted on her wedding day, then quickly excused himself to make a phone call.

Fifteen minutes later, the doorbell rang. For the first time in his life, Philip told the butler, "Don't bother, I'll answer it myself."

Having answered the door, he went to Elena's dressing room, where she was repairing the damage done to her makeup by the torrent of tears she had shed. He held out a peace offering.

"Darling, please forgive me. I hope that this small token of my love will make up for my having deserted you on the most important day of our life together."

Elena could see that the box was from Van Cleef & Arpels, and opened it with trembling fingers. Inside was a magnificent diamond necklace, each stone more beautiful than the next. As if that weren't enough, Philip placed two smaller boxes in her hands, one containing the matching diamond drop earrings and the other the two-inch-wide diamond bracelet that completed the set.

Philip gently adorned his wife with the priceless jewels, which only minutes earlier he had ordered to be sent immediately, from a company accustomed to dealing with the whims of the super-rich.

Elena was quite overcome by this instantaneous and generous gesture, but she was confused. He had ignored her the moment they were wed, and then acted like a bad little boy the moment she berated him—almost as though he enjoyed her abuse, and then wanted to impress her with his power to make it all better.

Once he was through covering her with diamonds, he brought out a box of chocolates and asked her to sit on his lap and feed them to him. She thought the request unusual, but did as he asked, while they talked baby talk to each other.

At seven-thirty they went in to a dinner that had been set up in the library—a room they felt would be more intimate than the massive formal dining room. This was where Elena had her first taste of one of the finest red wines in the world, from the Rothschild vineyards in France. Before the first sip, the newlyweds clinked glasses and said, "I love you, darling."

After dinner they retired to their room, where Elena waited for her wedding night to begin. Although they had never made a formal pact the way she had with Bruce, this would be the first time she and Philip were intimate.

Elena wasn't certain what she expected, but the whole experience lasted less than five minutes. No romance, brief penetration, and the sexual act was over.

Philip seemed unaware that something was missing; this was obviously his idea of lovemaking.

This was also the first time Elena had seen Philip without his full armor of clothing on. He had been completely shaved from his neck to his toes, and the only hair on his body was the little that was left on his head. Otherwise he was as bald as a baby. She was surprised.

"Darling, I've known fastidious men in my life, but never one who shaved every inch of his body," she said.

"It's easy, darling. Every morning, my masseur/valet, William, does it for me when I get ready for the day. It just feels so much cleaner."

The confused bride tried snuggling next to him.

Philip looked over at her and said, "You've made me very happy today, darling."

"Thank you for the beautiful gifts. You must have quite some influence at Van Cleef and Arpels to have them send such treasures within minutes."

"You don't need anything to make you more beautiful, but if they make you happy, then I'm happy."

With that said, Philip rolled over, opened the top drawer in his bedside table and started rummaging through bottles of pills.

"What are those?" asked Elena.

"My sleeping pills. Barbiturates, like Nembutal and Seconal. I also have a tranquilizer, Miltown; and uppers such as Tenuate or Benzedrine. Tenuates are really good for losing weight."

"But darling," Elena said, "it's our wedding night. How can you roll over and go to sleep? It's only ten o'clock."

"I always take a pill around now, and sleep for four hours. Then I wake up and walk around the house with a flashlight to see that everything is all right. After that I take another pill, sleep four more hours, get up, and start making phone calls to my business partners."

For Elena, who had never taken more than an aspirin in her life, this was just one more unexpected experience in this bizarre day.

Philip poured a glass of water from the silver carafe next to his bed and said, "Why don't you try one, darling? You'll sleep like a baby. And if you have trouble waking up, take one of these and you'll be fit for the day."

Elena was not used to sleeping at this early hour; she had always been more of a night person. But if she wanted to be on her husband's schedule, it seemed that her only choice was to take the pills.

"All right, darling, I'll try one tonight and see how it works."

"Don't worry, it'll work. Goodnight, darling."

Philip gave his bride a quick kiss, and then rolled over with his back to her and promptly went to sleep.

⁓

The next thing Elena knew, someone was shaking her and saying something about phone calls, the office, and other things that barely penetrated her semi-consciousness. Then it all came back to her. The wedding, the feeding of the chocolates as if to a little boy, the unsatisfactory lovemaking—and the pills—those god-awful pills that made her never want to get out of bed again.

"Here, darling, I have another pill to wake you up. You're obviously not used to them, but give them a chance. Here's some water and a Benzedrine. You'll soon be up and around."

Elena noticed that Philip was fully dressed and ready for his day. He would be going to the office, and all she would have were those damn pills to keep her company. She was not even going to have breakfast with her new husband. A brief kiss and he was gone.

Elena stayed in bed a long time that morning, sorting out exactly who this man was—this man she had thought she knew.

When she had berated Philip for deserting her on their wedding day, it was not the first time she had scolded him, but for the first time she had thought, My God, he's enjoying this. She was forced to accept that his reaction to her anger was part of the dark and sad side of his character that she had not wanted to face.

She realized that he had been given almost no love as a child; he had told her about the series of nurses brought over from France, each one called "Mademoiselle," who were the closest thing to a mother that he had ever known. These women did only what they were paid to do, nothing more. They could not afford to give of their heart: at any time they might have to leave and become "Mademoiselle" to a different lonely child.

The nurses had treated him as if he were a little god, the way he would later be treated as an adult in charge of the family business. At the same time, however, his father had expected them to chastise him for childish misbehavior, and the punishment had been carried out with either reticence or sadistic amusement, depending on which nurse was in charge. Disapproval was the only emotion the nurses had been allowed to express, and little Philip had interpreted it as love.

The thought occurred to Elena that Philip had been raised to be both a god and a sacrificial lamb. Her intuition told her that now, at this stage in his life when his only identity was his power, for a woman to keep his emotional interest she would have to treat him the same way he had been treated by the Mademoiselles. It was possibly the only kind of love that would keep him at her side for any length of time. No wonder all his other wives had given up so easily. Elena felt that she might be the one woman in the world who could cut through the dysfunction of her husband's upbringing.

She also thought about her family and how much they counted on her union with this man to provide them with everything they had ever dreamed of. How could she disappoint them?

At the same time, how could she deny that there was something about him that she adored? She wasn't even sure what it was, but from the start she had felt that Philip Zimmerman would be an important part of her destiny. She would try to make him understand what it meant to love and to be loved, no matter what the cost.

CHAPTER 8

Later that first morning after Elena's wedding night, when the wake-up pills had taken their full effect, she found herself feeling a certain euphoria that she had not expected, but that was quite pleasant. Once her brain had cleared enough for her to remember that Angelina was coming to stay, she rushed to prepare herself for the day ahead. She couldn't wait for Angelina to see the pretty pink and white bedroom she had decorated for her. She had even painted pink roses on the lampshades on either side of the bed.

Today they would go to enroll Angelina in Brearley, one of the top girls' schools in the city. Then they might do a little shopping, and go to the Central Park zoo to see the animals that Angelina loved so much.

It would be comforting for Elena to have her daughter with her in this enormous apartment. They had never been apart for long, and had shared their lives in a way that Philip would never understand. Elena was excited to show her that when either of them needed anything, all they had to do was ring the bell from whatever room they were in and a servant would instantly appear. It was a new way of life for both of them, and they would discover it together.

Once Angelina started school, though, life became lonely for Elena; she no longer had anyone to share her days with.

At night Elena took her pills with Philip, and she soon found that Tenuate in the morning not only gave her more energy and a sense of euphoria, but also cut her appetite, as he had suggested. Although she always had a perfect, slim figure, she was fearful of gaining weight. One of the most endearing things about her, for most men, had been that when faced with a large meal, the dainty, feminine Elena could chow down like a field hand. Of course she had never been sure how much longer she could eat that way without looking like her mother.

—

During the last few years Maria had lost her girlish figure, and had ballooned into a pretty but matronly middle-aged woman. Something tasty was always cooking in the oven, and the moment one walked into her house, her first question was, "Would you like some fried peppers?" It was an eternal mystery to her friends and family how tons of those damn peppers were always ready for frying. And they were good, too.

Soon after Maria moved back to Endicott, she ran into an electrician named Francesco whom she and Ernesto had known years ago. Francesco had always been in love with Maria, and was delighted when he heard that she was back in town. He was even more delighted to learn that Ernesto had gone to his eternal rest. Now he was free to make his move, and the next time Maria went to the grocery store, he bumped into her as if by accident.

"Maria, it's Francesco," he said. "You look more beautiful than ever, even with an armful of green peppers! I'm so sorry to hear about Ernesto. He was a good man—the best—God bless him—but if you should ever need a friend, I'd be happy to be there for you. Why don't you come by my little shop some day, Maria, and we can talk about the old days and how your three bambinos are doing?"

Never one to miss an opportunity, Maria made sure that their paths crossed again soon, and almost six months to the day after she buried her first husband, Maria and Francesco were married by Father Giovanni in the little Catholic church in Endicott.

—

Elena was alone so much of the time that she began to think that it might be nice to have her family living closer to her. Maria and her new husband readily agreed, as did Angelo and his wife, Lynn. It would mean a big jump in the world for them.

Elena soon found a charming one-bedroom apartment for Maria and Francesco on 72nd Street between Madison and Park Avenue. It was close enough for Elena and Angelina to walk to, if they so desired. But the best part for Maria and Francesco was that Elena would give them a generous allowance to pay their bills. As for

Angelo and Lynn, they were not shy at all, and moved right into the grand apartment on Park Avenue with Elena and Philip. After all, there was plenty of room for everyone. It was supposedly a temporary arrangement, but they stayed for a year.

During her first year of marriage, Elena had done her best to deal with Philip's erratic emotional behavior, but to no avail. She thought it might help to have Angelo and Lynn as buffers at the dinner table every night.

Elena was becoming dependent on the pills Philip had encouraged her to take. Now she needed two Tenuates to start the day and two more to cope with Philip when he came home at night. She could not go to sleep without endless rounds of Seconal or Nembutal—an indication of the stress this relationship was causing her.

Whether in spite of the drugs or perhaps because of them, Elena was still the charming, fun-filled, charismatic young woman who always showed her best face to everyone else. Even Angelina, Angelo, and Lynn had no idea how many of Elena's days were spent fighting despair and wondering how she had gotten herself caught up in this destructive environment. Maria and Francesco knew nothing about Elena's predicament, and were only concerned if a check did not arrive on time.

Elena finally confided in Angelo, "I see this emotionally childlike man walk in the door in the evening, and have to remind myself that to the people in the Zimmerman Building, he was a godlike creature when he walked in this morning.

"There's also no way I can make a real lover out of him. He truly believes that his 'wham bam' approach to lovemaking is every woman's dream. This kind of love is too much work and there is no guarantee of success no matter how hard I try. I'm tired, I'm exhausted, and I'm frustrated. I can also say that this is no way for Angelina to live. She's still a child and should not have to face the endless arguments Philip and I go through before he's satisfied that the little boy has been sufficiently punished. It's always abuse for him and then fabulous jewels for me. But what I really want is for the same man I go to galleries and antique stores with on Saturdays to come home to me at night after work."

Their strongest bond was their mutual love of beautiful things. The only times that Elena truly felt a union with Philip was when he took her to antique shops and galleries in the city; if they could have spent every day and every night roaming the city looking for priceless works of art, theirs would have been a perfect union.

Philip had great respect for her taste and judgment, and she never failed him. Their apartment was filled with the finest eighteenth-century French furniture and Impressionist paintings in the world—a gilded cage for a beautiful creature to exist in.

Despite her complaining to Angelo, during the early years of her marriage Elena worked hard to find ways to bring fun and laughter into Philip's life. She also tried to show him how normal family relations worked, using Angelo, Lynn, and Angelina as examples.

Friends started commenting about how much Philip had changed since his marriage to Elena. He was more relaxed and was beginning to appreciate the fun and joy that his wife did her best to infuse into their home. But even Elena could not change Philip's basic character.

The imperious mogul who spent his days at Zimmerman Investments was sometimes evident at home at night, especially when he entertained people who were beholden to him or who wanted him to will his massive art collection to their museum upon his death.

One evening Philip and Elena were entertaining an important business associate at a dinner party in their summer home on Long Island when their guest decided to tell a joke at the dinner table.

He said, "Someone asked a statue in Central Park, 'If you had one wish, what would it be?' The answer: 'Crap on a pigeon!'"

Philip went ballistic, and told the man, "Don't ever say anything so vulgar and disgusting in my presence again. If you think that's funny, well, I don't. I'm deeply offended and I hope you never speak that way in my house again."

The poor man was mortified in front of the other guests, and had no idea how to apologize appropriately. Elena was furious that Philip would have the bad manners to embarrass a guest in his home in such a haughty and rude manner. She said nothing at the time, but later, when everyone had gone home, she could not hold back, and thrilled Philip more than ever when she raked him over the coals for his unforgivable behavior.

The next day he came home with an emerald and diamond necklace, earrings, and bracelet from Van Cleef & Arpels, the way he had done on their wedding night. But it was getting too late in the game for her to be impressed by his attempts at buying her good will and then expecting her to sit on his lap and feed him more chocolates. Elena was exhausted and didn't know how much longer she could go on.

CHAPTER 9

Although Elena no longer stayed on Philip's "early to bed" schedule, she still took the pills, no matter how late it was when she finally joined him. Most nights she stayed up with Angelo and Lynn playing cards or watching television. After two years of marriage, Philip had told Elena, "I'm sorry, darling, but the tranquilizers that I take make it impossible for me to make love to you anymore. I hope you're not too disappointed."

Disappointed! She had been thrilled not to have to put up with faking orgasms on the infrequent nights when he spent five or six minutes doing what he thought of as satisfying his wife's sexual needs.

Bruce's lovemaking had been sweet but not earth-shattering, and after the traumatic revelations about him and his mother, Kay, the sexual act for Elena was always something to be endured, not enjoyed. But she was a good actress and no man had ever guessed that he had not made her divinely happy. What gave Elena pleasure was the sense of worth she felt when a man told her how enraptured he was by her beauty—the only thing she felt that she could still count on.

Elena's days now started with coffee and two Tenuates. Then she would dress and go out, roaming the shops, killing time until Angelina came home from school.

Rarely did Elena go to antique shops without Philip, but one day she came across a store she had not seen before. When she went in, she looked up and saw a beautiful man walking down a flight of stairs. He was tall and handsome with thick black hair, and he wore a suit that fit his trim torso like a glove. She stood still, staring at him.

The moment the man laid eyes on Elena, he stopped dead in his tracks. He had opened the shop because he loved exquisite objects, but this woman standing inside the doorway far surpassed any work of art he had ever been privileged to see in his life. She took his breath away. The attraction between the two was immediate and electric, and neither knew quite what to say.

Since he was the owner of the shop, he felt that it was up to him to make the first move. He walked down the stairs to where Elena stood motionless, took her hand, kissed it, and said in a thick Italian accent, "Welcome to my store, Signora, my name is Lorenzo Fioni."

That's all it took for these two to fall hopelessly in love.

Elena recovered her poise in time to say, "Thank you, Mr. Fioni. I look forward to seeing the magnificent objects you have in your store. I can see that you have good taste, from the beautiful things in your window."

"Please, Signora, call me Lorenzo. I feel as though we already know each other."

"Well, Lorenzo, my name is Elena, Elena Zimmerman."

"Ah, now I know who you are. I've seen your picture many times in the magazines and newspapers. Your husband is a famous man. But you, your pictures don't tell half the story. Yes, they show that you are beautiful, but they do not show the beauty of your soul."

Elena noticed that he was wearing a wedding band, and for just a few seconds she wished that she had not come into the shop. She sensed that meeting this man now would only cause her more pain than joy. However, for better or for worse, she knew that she wanted to know more, much more, about him.

The next day they met innocently enough for a long lunch, during which much wine was consumed. When it was over, they reluctantly went their separate ways, Lorenzo to his wife, and Elena back to her gilded cage.

That night, the wine, her feelings about Lorenzo, and the evening's Tenuates left Elena more frustrated about her relationship with Philip than usual. Everything her husband said or did irritated her, and dinner was a battleground. The others sat in mute silence throughout the painful meal.

Elena was in the library at bedtime, when Philip called her into their bedroom. He usually claimed that he was impotent because of the tranquilizers he took, but that night he was in a high state of sexual arousal after having been treated like a recalcitrant child during dinner. This was more than Elena could endure. That night it was impossible for her to go back to the games she had played to assuage Philip's arrested emotional and sexual development. She made a lame excuse about a female problem and rejoined Angelo and his wife in the library.

⌒

Several lunches later, Lorenzo closed the shop and let the saleslady go home for the afternoon. There was a small studio upstairs where he and Elena made love for the first time. It was a cozy room filled with objects d'art, and the perfect setting for the first real sexual experience of Elena's life.

Lorenzo undressed her slowly, kissing each part of her body as he uncovered it. When he took off his own clothes, one would have thought that two perfect Rodin sculptures had been placed in the room. Elena was longing to give herself totally to this lovely gentle man who looked at her with true love, mixed with a healthy dose of lust. His whole attention was on her, and for the first time she felt no need to act. Her emotions were too powerful. The one night she had spent with Bruce paled in comparison to the lovemaking that she was experiencing now, with a selfless man who received his greatest pleasure from pleasing the woman he loved.

That day he taught her how to enjoy every part of their bodies any way they wished. Mouths were not just for kissing on the lips, but also for giving endless pleasure in other places. Elena felt as though she had come out of a deep sleep and into a sensuous awakening.

Afterwards, they lay together in a state of pure contentment. Lorenzo had uncovered a passion that Elena had never known existed, and she had finally become a woman in every sense of the word.

He looked down at her upturned face and said, "If we never had to move from this position I would be the happiest man in the world. I could hold you in my arms forever."

"But Lorenzo, I'm yours. Nothing can part us."

Lorenzo hesitated for just a moment—long enough for Elena to feel the cold edge of fear in her soul.

"Elena, my beautiful Elena, if only you knew how much I want to be with you forever, but there are things about me you know nothing about. Parts of my life that have imprisoned me in a world I cannot escape from."

"Oh, Lorenzo, I understand what a prison feels like. I've been in one for longer than I care to remember. But now there is us and no one can take that away. I know you're married and so am I, but we'll find a way."

"My beautiful Elena, you don't really understand. Yes, I'm married, but in name only. Twelve years ago my wife, Mirella, and I were both content to agree upon a divorce until we found out that she was pregnant with our first child. We decided that we should stay together until the baby was born. But a terrible thing happened to the baby. My son, Fabrizio, was born with the umbilical cord wrapped around his neck, preventing his brain from receiving enough oxygen. As a result he was born with such severe brain damage that he is not able to speak or care for himself in any way.

"In spite of this, my wife and I love him very much and made a promise to each other that we would live together and care for him as long as God wants him on this earth. Some people say that we should put him in an institution, especially since he sometimes becomes violent. But for us, that is not an option. God gave him to us to care for and that is what we must do.

"So, my lovely Elena, that is the story of the prison I have lived in for more than twelve years. I hope you understand and can still love me enough to give me the only real joy I have found in this life—the joy I found the day I met you."

"Lorenzo, I am so sorry for you and your wife, and I admire you both for accepting the difficult task of caring for a child like Fabrizio. But you and I will somehow find our happiness without hurting anyone."

That night, dinner at the Zimmermans' was a joyous affair for Elena, who was in a mood of subdued elation. She felt complete and there was nothing Philip could do to upset her. He could be imperious, childlike, or servile, and she was able to let it all pass over her head. It was as though nothing mattered but Lorenzo, who had made her feel that she was more than just a beautiful creature that others could admire and use for their own purposes.

Elena was startled out of her reverie by Philip's voice at the other end of the dinner table. "Darling, I don't understand. Why did you say that you no longer need the car and chauffeur I put at your disposal every day? How on earth will you get around town?"

"Oh, Philip, don't be silly. I don't need all of that when I can just take a taxi like everyone else. It's so difficult for him to find parking spaces. When I go out I'm left standing in front of Bergdorf Goodman or Saks

Fifth Avenue while he's somewhere riding around the block."

Elena was not stupid, and knew at once that Philip wanted her to have the car and chauffeur so the driver could report all of her activities to him. She also knew that Philip was not stupid, either, not enough to completely trust his lovely wife to stay out of mischief while he spent long hours at the office every day.

⌒

Both Elena and Lorenzo knew that they could not stop this passion that existed between them. But if it were to continue, they needed a place of their own to be together. Elena immediately started searching for the perfect love nest and soon found a pretty ground floor studio apartment in a townhouse on 74th Street between Madison and Park Avenue. The location was conveniently close to both his shop and her apartment. There was even a small private garden out back. Of course, between the two of them they turned the small space into a jewel, with antiques that they uncovered in the back of Lorenzo's store.

Every day at noon Elena left her apartment, which by now she and Philip had filled with museum-quality pieces, and met Lorenzo at their apartment on 74th Street. They often made love and occasionally talked the afternoon away. But no matter what they did, their time together always started with a scotch on the rocks. They found a deep comfort in each other's company—a comfort that blotted out, at least for a while, the realities that dictated their lives once they parted.

When the butler opened the door to the Zimmerman apartment for Elena, her first words were always, "Good evening, Alan—a scotch on the rocks please. Is Angelina home yet?"

"Yes, Madam, right away. And Miss Angelina is in her room doing her homework, I believe."

The pattern was set. There was no way she could get through the evening without her Tenuates, her scotch and her barbiturates—three things she had known nothing about before Philip—a lethal combination at best.

～

When Elena went to her mother's house to tell her of the happiness that she had found with Lorenzo, Maria was apoplectic.

"How dare you endanger all our lives with a fleeting and cheap affair? Of course you're not happy in your marriage, because you cheat on your husband."

For the first time in her life, Elena openly defied her mother. "If you ever say anything like that to me again, I will never visit you again. I've finally found some happiness that didn't depend upon your or my brother's security in life and I will not let any of you take that away from me."

Maria knew when to be quiet, and this was one of those times. Both she and Angelo were completely dependent on Elena's generosity. Silence reigned in the living room as the plump lady rocked on the couch and pondered how to save the goose that laid the golden egg.

She didn't know whether Carlo received money from Elena, or not; he was a doctor with his own medical practice, and was now married to a woman named Bea—who, even Maria noticed, looked like a bad copy of Elena—but neither he nor Elena would ever say if she had helped him get established.

Maria, still uncharacteristically quiet, waited until she could see that Elena had calmed down a bit, and advised, "Honey, just don't ever let him catch you."

~

The only one who survived the erratic goings-on in the family relatively unscathed was Angelina, who by the age of twelve had begun to develop a mature figure with a breast size any grown woman would kill for. She had a unique look about her that resembled many of the sixteenth-century portraits so treasured by the Zimmerman family.

When Elena told her daughter about Lorenzo, Angelina was characteristically accepting of the situation, and happy that her mother had found some joy in her life. The day that Elena took Angelina to meet Lorenzo, the girl was surprised at how much she liked him, and told her mother, "You could have made a much worse choice."

By now Angelina had developed a good relationship with her stepfather. He not only gave her his name, but also asked her to call him "Daddy." This brought an emotional stability to her life that she had never known before.

Her grandmother lived nearby and was always happy to see Angelina when she came to visit. Nana's house was a comforting refuge for the girl. Life was simple there, and fried peppers were always welcome. Whatever Maria's failings and ambitions might have been, she loved her children and her only grandchild with all her heart.

For once, the whole family seemed truly content: Maria and Francesco were living on the generosity and reflected glory of the Zimmerman name; Angelina had someone to call Daddy; and Angelo and Lynn were happily living in the grand manner he had always believed he was entitled to—Philip had bought a two-bedroom apartment for them to use, in the same building he and Elena lived in. It was a clever way to keep them close by, and increasingly indebted to him. The couple knew that dinner upstairs with the Zimmermans was a definite requirement when Elena and Philip were home.

Whenever reporters asked Philip, "Mr. Zimmerman, what is your most priceless treasure?" he would answer, "My wife."

But still, every night when Elena walked into the Zimmerman apartment, she faced a husband she had to find ways to punish in order to keep her marriage alive and support her family's way of life.

Maria had often called Elena "Rosie," because, she said, "My daughter could fall into a pile of shit and come up smelling like a rose."

Elena herself had said that she had a "little devil" sitting on her shoulder—a little devil that would protect her forever. She didn't realize that the little devil might not always be there for her.

CHAPTER 10

A beaming Elena burst into her daughter's bedroom before dinner one night in mid-October of 1954 and announced, "Angelina, honey, Philip and I just had a wonderful idea. How would you like to have a costume party at home for your thirteenth birthday? You could invite some of your friends from school and their boyfriends for a sit-down dinner. Afterwards we can have a small band to play for dancing. Wouldn't that be a fun way to celebrate?"

Elena didn't have to say more than that to convince Angelina that it would be one of the best nights of her life. Most of the young women Angelina knew already had either a steady boy friend or a special crush they would love to invite to a costume party at the Zimmermans' home.

Dinner that night was a happy affair, with ideas flying back and forth across the table. Even Philip got into the party spirit, excitedly making suggestions of his own to help make the evening a night to remember. "I know!" he said. "Why doesn't Angelina dress as Cinderella going to the ball? We could have a beautiful white gown covered in shiny beads made just for her. With that dress and a sparkling tiara on her head, she'll look like a real princess!"

⁓

One of Angelina's guests for the party was a girl called Lucy, who had a crush on a boy she had met at one of New York's pre-debutante parties. The boy, Jean-Paul Duval, who was also thirteen, came from a prominent French family whose name was known around the world. His parents had come to New York City from France during World War II, so Jean-Paul had been born and raised in New York. His father had opened offices in the United States to expand the family business.

When Jean-Paul went to pick up Lucy, his date for Angelina's birthday, he had no idea where the costume party was going to be held, but Lucy had told him that a car would be waiting for them. The Zimmermans had sent cars around the neighborhood to chauffeur Angelina's guests to their home. Lucy was a pretty girl, but she had chosen the unfortunate costume of a butterfly, which did little for a figure that still carried a certain amount of baby fat.

On the way to the Zimmerman home, they stopped on Park Avenue to pick up another girl, Ann, and her date. Ann, who had a slim figure and a lovely face, had cleverly dressed in a powder-blue tulle dress with gold stars attached to her shoulders and gown. The theme of her costume was the song "Stardust."

The girls had obviously gone all out in planning their costumes, but the boys were at that in-between age where costumes did not fit into the macho image they tried so hard to project. As for Jean-Paul, a tall, slim boy who had inherited his mother's fine, aristocratic features and thick mane of blond hair, he had not given much thought to a costume, but was proud to be dressed in his first dinner suit.

He was not particularly intimidated the first time he entered the Zimmermans' foyer, which was filled with some of the most famous paintings in the world. He had seen and lived in grand homes all his life, and easily accepted the fact that everyone in his circle of friends lived that way. Jean-Paul also was not particularly impressed by the Zimmerman name; it was only one among many famous names he had known in his young life. To him, the Zimmerman family was no different from other prominent people he often met at his parents' dinner parties, or when he went out with his parents in Paris.

Nevertheless, he wasn't a snob, and he had been devastated when he learned that his best friend at the exclusive private school he attended could not live in the same apartment building as he, because his friend's family was Jewish and the building was restricted. While it was true that Jean-Paul enjoyed a glamorous lifestyle amid beautiful surroundings, he was wise enough to recognize fascinating people from all strata of society. He could sit for hours in his grandmother's kitchen at her chateau in France and converse with the head cook, Marie Eugénie—a motherly woman with a large bosom a small boy could cry on when he was hurt, and listen to the wisdom that this simple but wise woman had to offer. He, like Elena, was interested in what people brought to the table as human beings—nothing more.

When Jean-Paul and the girls walked into the Zimmermans' home, he barely noticed the walls in the foyer, which were covered with a Van Gogh, a portrait by Ingres of a French princess, and a Matisse. Instead, his eyes went immediately to Elena Zimmerman, whose photograph he had seen in the newspapers a few days earlier: smiling radiantly for the cameras, she had been leaning over a sports car that was being raffled off at a charity gala. He had no idea that real life would be so much more impressive than a mere photo. Since this was her daughter's big night to shine, Elena herself wore a simple black cocktail dress with a slightly provocative slit up the side of her left leg, and a stand-up collar that showed just enough cleavage.

And then Jean-Paul saw the stunning Angelina at her mother's side, dressed in the most beautiful costume of the evening, with shoes especially made to look like Cinderella's glass slippers. Lucy, the round little butterfly, didn't stand a chance of winning Jean-Paul's heart.

The moment Jean-Paul walked into the apartment, Elena, with her incredible gift of intuition working overtime, leaned towards her daughter, pointed her finger at the young man, and said the prophetic words, "He's ours!"

—

Jean-Paul was sitting on a large blue velvet sofa underneath one of the famous Renoirs from the Zimmerman collection when Elena came in and sat down next to him. She put her scotch on the rocks down on the coffee table and said, "You know, Jean-Paul, two years ago we bought this cute, cuddly puppy who has since grown into a dangerous, overgrown monster. She's absolutely huge and will feed on anything and anyone. We have to be very careful when she's around people. Oh, I think I hear her now. She hates it when guests come to the house and ignore her."

Jean-Paul, who was not the most aggressive adolescent in the room, and was armed with only a glass of Coca-Cola, dreaded the thought of embarrassing himself by climbing up on a chair and squealing in fear when "the monster" arrived. He was braced for the worst, when a tiny black poodle came wobbling arthritically into the room.

The little dog staggered over to Elena, who gently picked her up in her arms and said, "Daisy, I'd like you to meet our new friend, Jean-Paul. Jean-Paul, this is the dreaded Daisy."

"How do you do, Daisy," said the boy, wiping the perspiration from his forehead and laughing at the joke.

Elena, who had already spotted his innate shyness, knew that her little prank would put him at ease. He was so at ease, however, that he returned the favor by putting down his Coca-Cola and picking up her scotch on the rocks as though he intended to drink it. That moment, as they say, "sealed the deal," and Elena knew that her intuition about the boy had been right. He was "theirs."

At dinner, which Philip and Elena did not attend but kept an eye on from afar, Jean-Paul was seated next to Angelina. Unbeknownst to him, mother and daughter had organized a last-minute change in place cards the instant they first saw him.

Angelina, who had lived all her life in the shadow of her charismatic mother, felt really beautiful for the first time. For once she basked in the light that she had always seen surrounding her mother. The boy seated next to her was polite, amusing, and completely attentive to her. And he liked her. She could tell. She was certain of it after dinner, when they went into the other room and danced together while Philip and Elena watched proudly from a discreet distance.

The evening was a success, and Angelina had found her first love. Mother and daughter spent hours talking into the night and planning how to get the shy boy back into their orbit as soon as possible. Of course Elena soon had their strategy all mapped out. It was really very simple.

During the evening, Jean-Paul had told Elena how much he loved musical theatre and that there was a certain star he particularly enjoyed, the glorious Helen Dawson, who had thrilled audiences for almost three decades. Her new movie was opening the next week and Philip and Elena had been invited to the premiere.

Elena, with Philip's blessing, suggested to Angelina, "Why don't you take our tickets and invite your new beau, Jean-Paul, to the premiere of the film? Daddy and I could let you have the car and chauffeur for the evening so both of you can walk down the red carpet with the other celebrities. It's even going to be televised. What a thrilling first date that would be!"

"Oh, Mummy, I know he'd love it. And so would I. Thank you for being so clever, to think up the perfect date for Jean-Paul and me. I can't wait to ask him, but I can't call too soon or he'll think I'm overanxious. I don't know how I can stand it, but I'll wait a couple of days."

A couple of days seemed like forever, but Angelina needn't have worried. The next day Ruth, one of the chambermaids, knocked on her door to say that a boy with a strange French name was on the phone asking to speak to her.

Of course it was Jean-Paul, who wanted to know if she was going to attend the weekly William De Rham dance class that Saturday night at the River House. It was a dance class and a party all rolled into one. All their friends would be there, and Angelina had hinted that her parents were going to enroll her for the rest of the season. He was thrilled to know that she would be joining the group and neither of them could wait for Saturday night to come around.

After talking for a long while, Angelina said, "How would you like to go to the premiere of Helen Dawson's new film next week? Daddy is on the board of directors of the studio that produced the film, and he and Mummy offered to give us their tickets for the opening."

Jean-Paul couldn't believe his good fortune—a date with Angelina and the opening of a Helen Dawson film, all at the same time. He had never seen his idol on the stage, but a television special the year before, when he had first heard that magical voice and seen that indomitable personality on the small screen, had thrilled him in the deepest part of his soul.

All he could say was, "I can't wait. You and Helen Dawson are more than I ever could imagine in one evening. I'd love it. Thank you!"

—

When the evening arrived, Jean-Paul showed up at the Zimmermans' home before Angelina was ready. Elena, knowing her daughter was spending extra time making herself as beautiful as possible for her big date, was in the library, ready to greet the boy and make him feel at home.

Soon Angelina showed up in a beautiful red and black satin dress her mother had loaned her to wear for this special evening.

Needless to say, the premiere was a huge success. Jean-Paul was thrilled when, just before the lights went down, the beloved Helen Dawson took her seat nearby. It was like a fairy tale for the two teenagers, who basked in the glamour of the moment and the excitement of being with each other.

From that day forward, Jean-Paul became a permanent fixture in the Zimmermans' home. Weekends were spent with his new "family," and when Christmas vacation came around, they took him to Palm Beach with them for the New Year. Most of the time Elena, Angelina, and Jean-Paul were together, while Philip kept himself busy with business appointments. It seemed to suit Philip, who treated the boy as a son, to have someone to amuse Elena and Angelina when he was too busy to be with them. Jean-Paul was a perfect companion and escort and more than happy to play the part.

His mother was somewhat jealous of the relationship between him and the Zimmermans, particularly Elena; but she also felt that having her son be such an important part of the famous Zimmerman family was a feather in her Lily Daché hat.

—

By the time Jean-Paul was thirteen, when he met the Zimmermans, he was pretty savvy about pleasing the adults. He had impeccable manners, a sense of humor, and a deep appreciation for extraordinary and gifted people, but his most appealing trait was the sweet naiveté of a true born sophisticate. He had no false airs about him and was drawn to each of the Zimmermans for their own unique qualities.

He admired Elena for her total awareness of everything and everyone around her. She missed nothing. As far as Jean-Paul was concerned, her beauty was only a small part of the charismatic, compassionate woman who immediately recognized him as a kindred soul.

Mr. Zimmerman was harder for him to understand, but the mogul's unfailing politeness and generosity completely charmed the boy and put him at his ease. Even on the rare occasion when he felt that the older man looked right through him, it did not disturb Jean-Paul. He was smart enough to write it off as an adult aberration that had nothing to do with him.

As for the lovely Angelina, he couldn't believe his good fortune at having someone he could love without any pretense. They were walking on Worth Avenue in Palm Beach during a holiday break when Angelina suddenly grabbed his hand as they crossed the street. In that moment a current passed between them and he knew at that tender age that this was what love should always feel like.

CHAPTER II

"Elena," screeched Maria over the phone, "honey, I just spoke to Angelo and he told me that you still have this lover called Lorenzo. Jesus, Mary, and Joseph, you're going to ruin us all if you don't stop with this foolishness and be faithful to your husband."

"I love Philip, Mother. But I don't know how I could go on without Lorenzo. He brings light into my life."

"Let Philip light your life, and don't endanger everything you've got for a little fling."

"You mean 'don't endanger everything you and my brothers have'—and it's not a 'little fling.' I must go now. Please excuse me, Mother. I really must run."

"Oh, yes, I know where you're running to. Just remember, we finally made it, and you're no spring chicken anymore. 'Bye, honey."

"No spring chicken anymore…" "No spring chicken anymore…" The words ran through Elena's brain over and over, like a mantra. It was true that she was thirty-seven. Who would want her when she started to fall apart? She could already see subtle changes in her face and body—nothing anyone else might detect, but they were there. Once her beauty was gone, she would be of no use to anyone. Her life would be over. All day she sat in her room thinking about her mother's words. "You're not a spring chicken anymore." The pills and scotch helped her get through the day, but only barely.

～

"Philip, do you think that you could ask around and see if you could find a job for Angelo? I'm sure he'd be wonderful at something like public relations," Elena said to Philip one evening.

"Certainly, darling, I'll make some calls tomorrow."

What Elena did not know was that both Angelo and Philip were content with the way things were: work, to Angelo, was just another four-letter word, and Philip enjoyed having Angelo at his beck and call. It took the pressure off him, to have someone that he could trust to keep his wife busy, happy, and out of trouble when business took his attention away from family and home. He also knew that if Angelo got a job, the only way to keep him under his thumb would be to make sure that he did not make enough money to be independent. Either way, Philip still held all the cards.

He decided not to get a job for Angelo, but he did make sure that his brother-in-law and his wife had everything that they needed. Shopping was Lynn's passion, while her husband was occupied with his own amusements.

When everyone was busy and Angelina was at school, Elena continued her afternoons with Lorenzo. She took great pride in cleaning their little apartment herself and planting flowers in the garden. It made her temporarily feel like the one thing she had always said that she wanted to be: "a housewife."

Elena had believed since childhood that her only real asset was her physical appearance, so it was hard for her to accept that Lorenzo had fallen deeply in love with her for who she was. But he had—not only because of her looks, which helped, but also because of the compassionate, funny, and bright woman that she had always been.

One downside to their relationship was the additional scotch that she was drinking during their long afternoons together. Now she needed the alcohol and drugs to anesthetize her insecurities and her overwhelming feelings of responsibility to a family who counted on her to keep them in clover. It was like a knife in her heart each time they reminded her that it was her beauty that was keeping them all afloat.

However, as long as her family was receiving a monthly check, they had no complaints—especially not Maria, who was happy to see that her beautiful daughter's photos continued to be in the society magazines.

~

As their teen-age years went by and Angelina and Jean-Paul graduated from high school, the young couple slowly started to drift apart. They had been together for all of their years growing into adulthood, and the relationship was beginning to stifle them both. There was a world out there that neither had explored. Over the years, they had become more good friends than lovers. So far, Jean-Paul's excuse to Angelina for not being an enthusiastic lover had been that except for mild "petting," boys and girls were expected to behave themselves; it was not yet a promiscuous era.

The "breakup" was so amicable that they had dinner together with Elena and Philip the day they decided to "divorce," as Angelina put it. Elena and Philip were not upset, since Jean-Paul was like a son to them, one who would always be a part of their lives.

As for Jean-Paul, his behavior was dictated by the mores of the times. Although he loved Angelina, he had known since the age of five that he really preferred men to girls—something utterly shameful in the era he grew up in. No matter how hard he prayed for it to go away, it never did. It was the way God had made him, and he felt doomed to a shameful and hidden existence.

Elena was the one person in his life he might have been comfortable enough to unburden himself to, but even that was too frightening to contemplate.

And then there were his parents, who would never have accepted the shame of a gay son. For them, those people were flamboyant perverts that one could laugh at but never accept, especially in one's family.

Ever since he was a child, Jean-Paul had hoped for a career in show business. First he thought he wanted to be a pianist. Then, at the age of seven, he decided to be a ballet dancer. As a teen-ager, however, he finally realized that his greatest passion had always been singing and acting; his pretty soprano voice had matured into a very impressive high baritone.

When the time came for him to tell the Zimmermans of his plans to skip college and go into show business, Elena was very supportive and said, "You should follow your dream and do what makes you happy."

Philip, on the other hand, thought the idea outrageous and told him, "All actors are bums. It would make much more sense for you to go to Yale and then join me at Zimmerman Investments."

Jean-Paul was polite, as always, but knew in his heart that Yale and the Zimmerman offices would never be on his agenda. He also didn't believe that some business people were not worse bums than any actors he had known.

Shortly after leaving high school, he bought one of the trade papers that advertised open auditions— auditions anyone could go to. That's how he got his first job in summer stock. Entering the world of show business also turned out to be a good way for Jean-Paul to discreetly enter the underground world of homosexuality that existed in the 1950s. For the first time in his life, he was surrounded by others who were just like himself, which was comforting.

Angelina decided that she would like to go to school abroad; it would be a perfect chance to be on her own for the first time in her life. She loved languages and hoped to learn to speak German and to become more fluent in French. The Zimmermans soon selected a school in Switzerland for her. Before long she met a boy her age in Zurich and surprised no one in her family when she announced that she was seeing him exclusively; that had always been her style. Jean-Paul only hoped that her new friend was good enough for her.

With Angelina at school in Switzerland, Jean-Paul in summer stock, and Angelo and Lynn occupied with their apartment, Elena was on her own.

—

Soon after Angelina had left for school, Elena was waiting for Lorenzo at their apartment, sipping her first scotch of the afternoon, when the phone rang. It was Lorenzo. She had never heard him crying before.

"Darling, what's the matter? What happened?"

"It's Fabrizio. I can hardly say it. He's gone. My son is gone."

"What do you mean, 'he's gone'? Please calm yourself and tell me what happened."

"It was his heart. It just gave out during the night. The doctor says that it must have been a congenital defect that no one ever suspected. Mirella is sick with grief. We loved him so. Even with his damaged brain, he was a gift from God."

"Please, Lorenzo, come to the apartment. I want to share this terrible tragedy with you. You're not alone. I love you. Your pain is my pain."

"No, Elena, I'm sorry, but there are so many arrangements to be made and Mirella needs me to take care of her in her immense grief. Fabrizio was our baby, always our baby. And he gave us so much love. I'm sorry, but I promise to call you later. Goodbye, my Elena."

Elena sat impatiently by the phone, waiting for just a word from her lover. Finally, after five days, the phone rang. Her hands were shaking so much that she could hardly hold the receiver. Elena had a strong intuition about everything and everyone, and this was no exception. She tried to brace herself for what she knew was coming.

A strangled voice at the other end said, "Elena. I'm sorry that I haven't called sooner but... Oh my God!... How do I say this? I love you so much, but I must take Mirella back to Italy and her family. I'm afraid she's going to lose her mind with grief. She needs me, my darling, and I can't leave the mother of my child alone now. Please understand. Maybe someday we can be together, but right now I can't even bear the pain of seeing your lovely face before I go. Goodbye, my beloved."

Elena cried out, "Lorenzo—" but the phone was already dead. Elena was numb with pain. She understood what Lorenzo must do, but why must she also pay such an awful price, with no one to share it with? She sat in the little apartment waiting all afternoon, but she had nothing to wait for.

Then she thought of her mother, just a few blocks away. Elena was heartbroken, but she knew that her mother would secretly be happy—with Lorenzo gone, so was the danger to the lifestyle that the family had grown used to. In any case, she knew that her mother loved her and would at least be someone to hold her in her arms while she cried. Maria was not a stupid woman, and gave Elena the comfort she needed.

The pain was still there, but Elena was able to go home that night without having to put on a good face for Philip, since he was mercifully out of town on a business trip. At least Angelo and Lynn would come to the apartment for dinner, and were two people she could talk to.

That night Angelo gave his sister her sleeping pills, but slipped the bottle into his pocket. Once she dozed off, he removed all other medication from her room. He was not taking any chances.

⁓

It took some time before Elena rallied—but she rallied in her own way. She hired a famous decorator to help her redo the library. He was not gay, and took it upon himself to comfort Elena as much as he could; he was more than happy to be her lover. Soon there were others; it no longer mattered where they came from. Having a man make love to her was like an anesthetic.

Lovers, booze, and pills were all that she had to help her survive.

During one of Angelina's visits, Elena told her, "So many men have told me that they want to be with me when I'm old and sick. They say that then they'll have me all to themselves. But darling, I know better. They'll all be gone by then."

Jean-Paul, who had been sitting nearby, overheard the conversation between mother and daughter and thought, I won't desert you. I'll always be there for you.

CHAPTER 12

In the summer of 1969, Elena was fifty years old, although she had never quite believed it would be possible for her to be that old. A little nip and tuck over the years had kept her looking as youthful as ever, but she no longer felt young. The men she needed in her life to validate her worth were now more gigolos than lovers, and she was willing to pay for their validation.

There was no longer any chance of her being "just a housewife." She was drowning in a pit of loneliness that she had fallen into many years before, when she had sold herself to a man who could provide everything her family wanted from her. And the pit had only gotten deeper with the loss of Lorenzo, her great love.

That summer Angelina was in California, where she, rather than Elena, was the one who relished the role of a happy suburban housewife with her husband of four years, Mark, and their three-year-old son, Gregorio.

Meanwhile, Jean-Paul was doing a concert tour of the East Coast with great success, and the Zimmermans were on Long Island, where Elena spent her days alone with Angelo and Lynn. Philip, of course, took the yacht into the city five days a week to be in his office at the Zimmerman Building.

Although Elena still thought about Lorenzo every day of her life, she had no choice but to face the fact that she might never see him again.

She told Angelo and Lynn, "The only thing I can do is accept that all I might ever have are my memories. I don't even know where he and Mirella are living—somewhere in Italy, I suppose. I admire his devotion to duty, but I can't help but feel a loss.

"I also wish I could stop those damn pills and get through just one day without the scotch, but I can't. They help me to survive as best I can. I have all the money any woman could use, jewels fit for a queen, beautiful homes, a yacht, and more couture clothes than I can ever wear, yet I pray just to hear Lorenzo's voice telling me 'I love you' one more time."

One Friday night after dinner, Philip, Elena, Angelo, and Lynn were in their private movie theatre watching a film that Metro-Goldwyn-Mayer had sent over for them to see before its release to the general public.

The four of them were sitting comfortably on the lounge chairs in the front row enjoying the movie, when Philip discreetly got up from his seat, leaned over to Elena, and whispered, "I just remembered an important business call I have to make before ten o'clock tonight. If you'll excuse me, I'll be back in a few minutes."

Elena, who was by far the most intuitive person in the room, smiled sweetly as her husband went out the door to go make his call in the main house.

She waited for a few moments and then quietly got up and made her way in the semi-darkness to the main house. She tiptoed upstairs, and when she heard Philip on the phone in his room, she went to her own quarters and quietly picked up an extension to listen in on her husband's conversation.

She heard Philip say, "Georgette, I never thought I'd be able to get away and call you tonight. It was wonderful being with you this afternoon. I can't imagine what a thirty-year-old woman like you sees in a man nearing his eighties like me. I never thought I could make such passionate love again, but we did."

Then Elena heard a woman with a French accent say, "Oh, Philip, you're the best lover in the world. I never dreamed I would find a man as wonderful as you. It doesn't matter how young I am or how old you are, we have this wonderful moment to share and the time to be together. Your wife need never know what goes on in the afternoon when she thinks you're at the office."

Elena's worst nightmare had finally come true. A younger woman had taken her place. She was old now, her looks would soon be gone and no one would want her anymore. That, for Elena, was the end of the world. What was to become of her and her family? She had done everything she could to meet their expectations. Elena had found comfort in her relationship with Philip, and security in knowing he would take care of them all. But she never allowed herself to think it was due to anything but her beauty. Now she knew it was over.

Elena silently hung up the phone and walked into the hallway between their bedrooms. There she met Philip, who was on his way back to the movie.

At first he looked shocked to see her. Then he saw the look on her face and he knew.

"Philip, how could you?"

"You heard it all then."

"I heard enough."

"Don't misunderstand me, Elena. It's nothing but an old man trying to regain his youth."

"So I'm too old for you now. Is that it?"

"Elena, no! Listen to me…"

"Philip, it's very simple. I want you to give that woman up."

"I can't. I love you, Elena, and I always have, but she makes me feel young again."

He knew the moment he said it that Elena was too insecure to be able to tolerate that kind of answer.

She turned to run into her room, lost her footing, and tumbled to the bottom of the stairs, where she struck her head on the base of a Giacometti sculpture.

Angelo and Lynn, who had wondered what Elena was up to when she slipped out of the theater to follow

Philip, had a premonition that it would be best to go back to the house and see what was going on. They knew there was serious trouble the moment they saw Elena lying unconscious on the floor, with blood pouring from her head.

"Thank God, you're both here. Elena heard me on the phone with another woman and confronted me. We had a terrible row. The next thing I knew she reeled around to go back to her bedroom, then stumbled and fell to the bottom of the stairs. Angelo, please call for an ambulance right away. We have no time to lose."

~

The hospital waiting room was a grim place to be. All anyone could do was wait to hear the good or the bad news about a loved one. Angelo, Lynn, and Philip sat silently while the doctors worked to save Elena's life.

Finally a doctor came to them and said, "I'm Dr. Goldman. Mr. Zimmerman, I'm sorry, but your wife is in a deep coma right now. Fluid is rapidly building up around her brain from the trauma to her head, and our only choice is to operate to relieve the pressure. There's no way for us to know at this time if she will be left with any permanent damage to the brain."

Philip seemed to take it all in, but when the doctor had left he turned to Angelo and said, "What happened? Why are we in this place? I can't seem to remember how we got here. Is this a hospital? Where's Elena?"

"Philip, Elena fell down the stairs at the house and hurt her head, but the doctors are taking good care of her. I'm sure that she'll be all right."

Meanwhile Lynn ran up to Dr. Goldman to tell him what had just occurred with Philip.

The doctor took a confused Philip into his office and examined him. After a few minutes, Philip's vital signs were normal and he seemed to be regaining his memory.

"In my opinion, Mr. Zimmerman, the stress of this whole evening has caused the little episode you just had. The strain was too much for a man of your age. I think what you need is a good night's rest. We'll keep you informed of your wife's condition and call you as soon as there is any change."

Lou, the caretaker, who had driven them to the hospital, was waiting outside to take them back home.

⌒

The next morning Angelo learned that there was no change in Elena's condition. She was still in a coma and there was no way of knowing what condition she would be in, if or when she regained consciousness.

First, Angelo called Maria, who was sure that if she prayed hard enough her daughter would be fine. Angelina insisted on taking the first plane from California to New York to be with her mother. Then Angelo called Jean-Paul, who was beside himself with frustration that his contracts would not allow him to leave his tour and be at Elena's side. He had always believed that Elena was a superhuman woman who could overcome anything, and he found it impossible to fathom that she could no longer do so.

Everyone knew that the next few days would most likely seal Elena's fate. Each day that went by diminished their hope for her recovery.

Finally, on the sixth day, with Angelina at her side, Elena opened her eyes. She tried to speak, but no one could understand her.

When she had regained full consciousness, it was evident to the doctors that she had suffered an injury to the motor portion of her brain. Her intellect was intact, but her speech was garbled and sounded like that of a very drunken person. And when they tried to make her walk, she was unsteady and lost her balance—again, like someone who was drunk.

Angelina stayed as long as she could, but soon had to go home and take care of her family. Jean-Paul was devastated by the news that his beloved friend would never be the same again and was dismayed that he could not be with her. He was grateful to Angelo, however, for the daily telephone updates on her condition, even though it never seemed to improve.

One day Jean-Paul asked, "How is Nana"—that's what he called Maria—"taking the news of Elena's condition?"

"Well, Jean-Paul, Mother is doing very well. As a matter of fact, she's relieved that Elena is too incapacitated to endanger her relationship with Philip anymore."

Jean-Paul was horrified at the old woman's pragmatic response to her daughter's condition.

~

Because of the Zimmerman name, Elena was not made to seek help in dealing with her physical problems. Instead they were shoved aside. She managed to tell her doctor, "If I can't talk, then I won't talk."

As soon as Philip could, he had his wife moved to Columbia Presbyterian Hospital in New York City, since it was closer to home. Elena stayed there for two months. During that time her only diversion was when her hairdresser/makeup man, Dan, came to make her beautiful. Every night she would ask the nurse to comb out her hair and wash her face, so he could start all over again the next day. Philip paid the man a fortune every day, but having Elena's hair and makeup done was the one thing that he knew would give his wife some comfort.

—

A few days before Elena was scheduled to come home from the hospital, Angelo received a call from Philip's office. The secretary said, "I'm sorry to have to tell you this, Mr. Manziano, but Mr. Zimmerman is on his way to the hospital. It seems that he had a stroke in the middle of a meeting. His lawyer is with him. I'm sure Mr. Zimmerman would want you to know so that you can break the news to his wife."

"Thank you, I'll be right there. Is he also at Columbia Presbyterian Hospital?" Angelo asked.

"Yes, sir. Again I'm sorry to bring you the bad news, but we all hope he'll soon be fine. Goodbye."

—

"Gentlemen," said the doctor to Philip's lawyer, Seymour Perlstein, and Angelo, "as you must know by now, Mr. Zimmerman has had what is commonly called a stroke. At the moment he cannot speak and it is difficult for us to evaluate him completely. Once we are certain that there is nothing more we can do for him here, he has the resources to have physical therapy and be well cared for at home. Now, has someone notified Mrs. Zimmerman of her husband's condition?"

"Yes, Doctor," said Angelo. "She is aware of the stroke and that he is in the same hospital as she is. By the way, do you think it possible that the 'episode' Mr. Zimmerman had with his memory when his wife was first admitted to the hospital in Long Island is connected with what happened today? Could it have been a smaller stroke or a sign of what was coming?"

The doctor tactfully answered, "Mr. Manziano, without having been there myself, it's impossible for me to evaluate what Mr. Zimmerman's condition was on the night in question. If that is all, gentlemen, I have some other patients to attend to."

—

When Elena went home, Angelo hired a woman to live in the apartment and help her with her special needs. Naturally, Dan the hairdresser/makeup man was also there every day.

Mr. Perlstein, the power closest to the Zimmerman throne, made arrangements to turn a room at the Zimmermans' apartment into a mini-hospital for Philip to come home to. Philip was a powerful man who controlled much of the world's business, but he was powerless against the spectre of death, and it terrified him. He believed that if a doctor and nurse were with him at all times, he would be certain to live forever; and he could afford to hire as many doctors and nurses as he wished to stay by his bedside twenty-four hours a day.

Angelo and Lynn no longer felt an obligation to go to dinner every night with Elena, and there was now no need to try to make points with Philip at dinnertime. They would look in on him once a day, but that was all.

Jean-Paul, on the other hand, rushed back to New York to be at Elena's side as soon as his tour was over. She had already been home for a couple of months, and Angelina had just come in from California to visit for a week.

When Jean-Paul called Angelina, she said, "Late this afternoon, Angelo, Lynn, Mummy and I are all going to Nana's house for a visit. Why don't you come to the apartment earlier, so we can all go to Nana's together?"

He was apprehensive at meeting Elena for the first time since her accident; he was not sure what to expect. According to Angelo, her speech and her walking had not improved, and she would undoubtedly stay this way for the rest of her life. Jean-Paul's greatest concern was how she would feel about his seeing her in this condition.

When he arrived at the apartment, Angelina met him at the front door, threw her arms around him, and then led him into the library—a room that held so many memories for them both.

"Here comes Mummy now. We should be leaving right away."

Jean-Paul turned around and saw his exquisite friend walking slowly down the long hallway, holding on to Angelo's arm.

Angelo and Elena entered the library, where Jean-Paul kissed his old friend on the cheek and said, "You look as beautiful as ever."

He nearly died of embarrassment when Elena stumbled on a small carpet and fell to one knee. Angelo, who understood Jean-Paul's predicament, helped his sister up, and casually said to him, "Now, let's see. Lynn and I can go in one taxi, and you and Angelina and Elena can take another one. We'll all meet at Mother's house. Come on, everybody, or we'll be late."

Angelo smoothly transferred Elena's hand from his arm to the young man's. On the way over to Maria's house, Jean-Paul and Angelina chatted away, while Elena remained silent. Jean-Paul found it surprisingly easy to help Elena out of the taxi and up to her mother's apartment, without any awkward moments. Their movements were like a dance that had been well choreographed and rehearsed. Once inside the apartment, he sat on the sofa beside her.

Never once during the evening did Elena speak. Finally Jean-Paul turned to her and said simply, "I've missed you." She didn't answer, but her eyes became misty as she gently touched his hand with hers.

Nothing more was said until he kissed her goodnight at the door of her apartment, and left her in Angelina's care.

CHAPTER 13

❝ Hello, Jean-Paul, this is Angelina. I'm here with Mummy, and we wondered if you would like to come for dinner tonight. I'm going back to California tomorrow, and I'd love to see you again before I go."

"Hey, that sounds great! I hope it's okay, but I was going to have dinner with my manager tonight. I wonder if I could bring him along?"

"Of course, we'd love to meet him. How's seven o'clock? We can make some Margaritas and then have one of Nora's wonderful home-cooked dinners." Nora was the Zimmermans' longtime cook. "Just like old times. How's seven o'clock?"

"Seven it is. 'Bye."

Elena and Angelina still had no idea that "their" Jean-Paul was a gay man, and that his manager, Christopher Bianchi, had been his lover for the last three years. It was easy for them to get away with the relationship because they worked together. People may have suspected, but not even most of their closest friends knew the real story. Christopher had an apartment in New York City, and Jean-Paul stayed with his parents in between concert engagements.

Jean-Paul's mother, Jacqueline, had her own suspicions, but the haughty lady never mentioned it.

⁓

At seven on the dot, the two young men were at the Zimmermans' door.

Angelina met them in the foyer and said, "Mummy wants you both to come down to her room so we can have drinks there."

As they passed the first door on the right, Angelina whispered, "That's Daddy's room. I've never seen doctors or nurses, but they're with him all the time. Do you remember Lois, who used to work at the house in Long Island? She also comes in and sits with Daddy. She always thought he was the most wonderful man in the world, and she is especially devoted to him now."

Elena's room was at the far end of a long corridor, past walls covered with priceless artwork. The parquet floor had been flown in from a palazzo in Venice. This was the first time that Christopher had seen such opulence in a private home. The thought entered his mind, "How ironic. Everything in this apartment is of museum quality, and yet, of the two people who live here, one is crippled with a devastating stroke and the other is living with brain damage."

Although Elena was waiting for them with a drink in her hand, she no longer tolerated the daily scotch. Not only did liquor now have a stronger impact on her diminished capacities, but also the brain injury had calmed the need for her once-necessary anesthesia of pills and booze. She was wearing a beautiful Japanese kimono she had bought in Asia, and had a genuinely happy smile for the young group that surrounded her that night.

The minute Elena and Christopher met, they felt an instant rapport—almost as powerful as when Jean-Paul had first walked into her life. She talked little, but smiled and laughed with the others. She was enjoying herself for the first time since she had left the hospital.

Christopher could easily see Elena's charisma and magic, which had not been erased by the damage to her brain. That she was still beautiful was a given, and tonight the two gay men made her feel young again with their admiration and love.

—

From that night on, Jean-Paul and Christopher had an open invitation for dinner with Elena any time they wished, which turned out to be every night that they were in town. Her speech was difficult to understand, but they soon got used to it, in the same way that parents can understand what their young child is saying when no one else can decipher it.

Sometimes Elena would surprise them and say, "Why don't we go to the theatre tomorrow night? I'll get tickets and then we can go have dinner somewhere fun."

After dinner in the restaurant, Jean-Paul would inevitably say to Elena, "Come on, let's blow this joint," to which Elena, with a naughty twinkle in her eye, would respond, "You take that half of the room and I'll take this half of the room!"

When Jean-Paul asked Elena where Angelo and Lynn were, she said, "Now that Philip is bedridden, they never bother to have dinner with me anymore. When they do visit, it's to look in on Philip. If it were not for you two, I would be alone every night. You have given me life again."

One evening Jean-Paul asked Elena, "When do you go in and see Mr. Zimmerman?"

She shook her head sadly and said, "Never. He's embarrassed for me to see him in this condition. So I honor that."

Philip's care was watched over by his lawyer and his senior partners at Zimmerman Investments, Inc. The powers that sat near the throne before his stroke now sat on the throne.

By summer, Perlstein and his cohorts figured there was no reason for Philip to be moved to Long Island for the season; he would be just as comfortable lying motionless in his hospital bed in New York as he would in another one on Long Island. Elena was not consulted.

Jean-Paul was visiting Elena at the apartment when Lois, Philip's faithful caretaker, ran up to him in tears.

"Mr. Perlstein instructed me today that I am not to take care of Mr. Zimmerman anymore. In his opinion,

Mr. Zimmerman is getting too attached to me, and he wants me out of the house. How can he do that? I care so much for Mr. Zimmerman. I only want for him to be as comfortable as possible. Those people have no heart."

"No, Lois, they don't have any heart. They're paranoid about their own power. They believe that if Mr. Zimmerman gets too attached to you, it might give you some power to manipulate a dying man. I'm sorry, but that's the kind of vultures we're dealing with here. I'm afraid that you have no choice but to give in to them," Jean-Paul told her.

—

In April of 1970, Jean-Paul was doing some concerts in New York and was staying at his parents' home. One morning, Angelina called at nine, uncharacteristically early for either of them.

"Jean-Paul, I hate to tell you this, but in spite of his doctors and nurses around the clock, Daddy had a heart attack during the night and died within minutes. Mummy wants to know if you can come over to the apartment as soon as possible?"

"Of course, Angelina. Thank God you came two days ago to visit. How is your mother?"

"It's hard to tell. I think she's in shock. She proba-bly believed that Daddy would live forever—the way he did. You know how good she is at denial."

"I'll be right there."

When he walked into the Zimmerman apartment, Angelo was already there to greet him. Jean-Paul made his own way down the corridor to Elena's room, where she was lying in bed, with Angelina sitting beside her. He leaned over the bed, kissed Elena, and said, "I'm so sorry," and Elena answered, "So am I."

They all knew that he had to appear at a concert that night. Elena surprised him by asking, "Can I come with you tonight?"

At first he was startled by her request, with her dead husband only a few rooms away, but then he thought, If she doesn't come with us tonight, she'll be alone and de-pressed in this huge palace she and Philip called home. This way, at least she can be distracted for a little while from the reality of such a major loss in her life.

⌒

Philip Zimmerman's death was big news and made the front page of every newspaper in the country, in-cluding half the front page of The New York Times.

Power wars were sure to ensue at Zimmerman Investments, Inc.

The funeral was to be held at the original family mansion and was choreographed by none other than the lawyer Perlstein, who was gloating at his new importance in the scheme of big business.

Jean-Paul went to the Zimmermans' apartment early to pick up Elena and Angelina. He found that Elena's hairdresser was having trouble adjusting her heavy black veil without destroying her hairdo.

There was silence in the limousine on the way to the funeral, and Elena clutched her young friend's arm tightly as they passed by the swarms of reporters who were waiting outside the mansion. The fact that she was on the arm of Jean-Paul Duval brought even more attention to the two of them, but he was a pro at this sort of thing and guided her smoothly through the crowd.

The ceremony was to take place in a rather small room on the second floor, and after taking Elena to her seat on a red velvet sofa in the front row, Jean-Paul took a discreet seat a few rows behind her. No sooner had he sat down than Perlstein came up to him and asked in his smarmy way, "Would you mind standing? That seat has been reserved for General Omar Bradley."

Jean-Paul immediately stood up to make room for the elderly general.

The truth was that there was no room for anyone who was of no immediate use to Perlstein. Angelo, who had overheard the conversation, stepped in and said, "That's all right, you can have my seat, Jean-Paul." He knew that the lawyer couldn't throw Jean-Paul out of that one.

After the ceremony was over, Jean-Paul tried to make his way through the crowd, so Elena would have his arm to lean on. By the time he caught up with her at the elevator, a man who didn't know that he was accompanying the widow stopped him. Elena walked into the elevator with Angelina, and as the doors closed, the last thing Jean-Paul saw was Elena turning around, facing the back, and putting one arm over her face so she could weep in private.

Next to the elevator was a short flight of stairs, and Jean-Paul ran down them in a flash. His arm was ready for Elena to take hold of when the elevator doors opened on the ground floor. She gave him a little tearstained smile through her heavy veil that told him, "I knew you'd be here waiting for me."

That night Elena, Angelina, Jean-Paul, and Christopher had dinner together at the Zimmermans' apartment. Elena told them that Philip had left her some very important pieces from the collection; the apartment; everything in her bedroom (which was filled with works of art); a large portion of his interest in Zimmerman Investments, Inc. in trust (Philip understood that her generosity had no bounds); and millions in cash. All in all, Elena was now a very rich woman in her own right.

Jean-Paul asked Elena, "How do you feel about having this great wealth in your own name now?"

"I preferred it when Philip was here to take care of me. Now I'm alone with a very heavy responsibility."

—

One person who reveled in Elena's new status was Angelo, who now took it for granted that he would be in charge of Elena's fortune. His power and ability to spend would be limitless. He knew that Elena had no interest in or knowledge as to how to handle her money, so he told her, "Don't worry about anything, I'll take care of your money. There's no one that you can trust more than family, especially your brother, who's always been there for you."

Elena had spent her life pleasing her family, and blocked out the fact that Angelo and Lynn had not been there for her in the past year while Philip lay dying. In the end, it was inconceivable to her that her beloved Angelo would have anything but her best interest at heart. She had been raised to believe that family always came first, no matter what. And so she gave him the power of attorney over her affairs, as he requested.

Maria was beside herself with joy.

"Finally my baby is a rich woman in her own right, with everything one could desire, and my Angelo will take good care of us all." What she meant most sincerely was the "us all."

$\sim$

When Jean-Paul and Christopher decided that it was time for them to find an apartment together, each person in their intimate circle had a different reaction to the news.

Even Jacqueline came down from her ivory tower and gave them her seal of approval. For a woman who thought that ninety-nine percent of the world was "common"—including the Queen Mother of England, because she stood with her feet about two inches farther apart than Jacqueline thought was proper—it was surprising how much she liked her son's lover. Christopher came from a respectable Italian family in Connecticut, had perfect manners, handsome dark good looks, and had done marvels for her son's career. He also knew how to shamelessly flatter Jean-Paul's snooty mother until she turned into a simpering schoolgirl—a part of her that her son had never seen before. In any case, Jean-Paul was relieved that his boyfriend had passed Jacqueline's "common" test with flying colors.

Elena was delighted for them, and said, "That's wonderful! We can have fun decorating the place. I love decorating apartments and making them pretty."

It was hard for the young men to hold Elena's spending down because her generosity was boundless. She had great ideas about fabrics and colors, and insisted on buying some of the things she suggested, herself. The total that they allowed her to spend came to fifteen hundred dollars. Had the boys given her free reign, it would have been fifteen thousand. In the end, their apartment was beautiful—everything they could have expected and more.

When Angelo found out, rather than being happy for them, he seemed angry. Jean-Paul was puzzled by his reaction, but Christopher, who had observed Angelo with a more critical eye, said, "No, I think he is jealous of us and of anything, no matter how small, that Elena might spend on us."

⁓

When Thanksgiving rolled around, Jean-Paul finally realized that he had a problem with Angelo. For many years Jean-Paul had been considered as family and had always been invited to Maria's house to celebrate the holidays. But this year he received a phone call from Angelo, who said coldly, "I'm sorry, Jean-Paul, but there's no room for you at Mother's house this time. She's had cataract surgery and can't deal with too many people."

Jean-Paul, against Christopher's advice, decided to drop in at Maria's apartment anyway, to wish everybody a happy Thanksgiving, and then leave.

Elena was delighted to see him and had expected him to be there anyway.

"Hi, Nana, I only stopped by for a minute to say 'Hello' before I go to my mother's house to see my family."

He sat down next to Maria, who wasted no time saying, "I hear my daughter is giving you fifteen hundred dollars a month. I always thought you made good money. What do you need our Elena's money for?"

"Nana, none of it is true. Elena insisted on buying fifteen hundred dollars of merchandise to help decorate my new apartment. Nothing else. And no, I am not on her payroll—never have been, never will be!"

With that said, he went over to Elena, kissed her on the cheek, said goodbye to the others, and left. It had taken less than ten minutes. He didn't care if the old bitch Maria believed him or not, but at least now he knew the score.

~

During the next few months Elena had a ball traveling with Jean-Paul and Christopher wherever he was singing. The three of them even went on a trip to Hawaii after an engagement in British Columbia. The only problem they sometimes encountered was getting around with the twenty suitcases they carried among them.

Life was wonderful for Elena and "her boys." Laughter and fun was always on the agenda, and she always had Jean-Paul's arm to hold on to. It almost seemed too good to be true for the three of them.

Even Angelo and Lynn were having a good time. They were redecorating their apartment, which Elena had generously put in their name. They filled it with more furniture than a small department store. And after Elena gave them $500,000 so they would feel independent, they asked her if they could borrow a priceless diamond-covered box—it would make them feel special just having one priceless object sitting in their living room. Elena was able to oblige them since it was among the items that Philip had left to her. But it seemed that the more they were given, the more they wanted.

That summer, Angelo and Lynn thought it would be nice to hire a decorator to redo the house on Long Island. Elena, who had exquisite taste and had already decorated the house beautifully, was not consulted. Not only did Angelo and Lynn keep her a virtual prisoner there, refusing to allow Jean-Paul and Christopher to visit her, but they also turned the beautiful home she had created into a gaudy version of a cheap resort. The muted tones she had used on the Louis XV furniture were replaced with vivid reds and loud fabrics that took all the old elegance away from the home. Even Philip would have been horrified.

Angelo had built his castle and was now Lord of the Manor. He had waited his whole life for this moment, and he believed, as Philip had, that he was going to enjoy it forever. But nothing on this earth is forever.

CHAPTER 14

Shortly after Philip's death, Angelo started feeling discomfort in his abdomen. He had always been as strong as a water buffalo, and it took Lynn weeks to get him to see a doctor. Many tests were made before the doctor saw some irregularities in Angelo's liver. After more tests, the doctors told Angelo that, in their opinion, they needed to do an exploratory operation. However, like many people who have never been sick in their lives, Angelo was terrified of going under the knife.

He put on a good show of not being afraid of anything, but even so he only showed his face in Elena's apartment when he wanted her to sign checks. It was Lynn who told Elena how frightened he really was.

Months went by, and Angelo still hadn't had his operation. He could never commit to a date. He was too busy playing the role of the mogul and pretending that he was now Philip Zimmerman. He had no problem spending his sister's money, at the same time telling her that she was too extravagant.

One afternoon Elena, Jean-Paul, and Christopher were walking through the lobby of Elena's building when they saw Lynn waiting for the elevator. Angelo's wife looked close to tears, and she asked, "Can I go up to your apartment, Elena? I must speak to you about something."

"Of course, Lynn. Come on up with us."

Once inside the apartment, Lynn made it clear that Jean-Paul and Christopher were not welcome to be present for this conversation. The two men went discreetly into another room while Lynn and Elena spoke in the library. Jean-Paul understood that Lynn, who had been one of his best friends shortly after her marriage to Angelo, now believed her husband's lies about

Elena's generosity toward the boys. Angelo still rarely spoke to Jean-Paul, which was fine since their paths
hardly ever crossed.

After Lynn had left, Elena, of course, shared the story with her best friends, Jean-Paul and Christopher.

"Lynn told me that she just met with Angelo's doctors. They said that Angelo has terminal cancer. The disease has invaded his pancreas and his liver. Lynn doesn't
feel that Angelo is emotionally strong enough to deal
with the prognosis, so she begged the doctor to tell him
that he has hepatitis and therefore does not need an operation. The only thing for him to do is rest, and by the
summer, when the real suffering begins, we can have
nurses on hand to give him the morphine he'll need to
control the pain. We can probably keep up the charade
until it's over."

Later that afternoon, Angelo and Lynn paid a surprise visit to the Zimmerman apartment. Angelo was in
a rare good mood, while Lynn acted to perfection the
part of the happy little wife.

"You see, I was right," Angelo exulted. "Everything
ultimately goes my way. The doctors told me that I don't
need an operation after all. I don't mind telling you that
I didn't want that operation under any circumstances,

and now I find out that it isn't necessary. I just need to rest my liver for a little while and I'll be in as good a shape as I ever was. Elena knows that I was born under a lucky star. In a couple of months we can go to Long Island."

After a chorus of "That's wonderful news, Angelo— congratulations!" he and his wife retired to their home for the evening.

~

Within a few months, Angelo was on heavy pain medication, but he wanted to go to Long Island. He had to be transported by ambulance to the house that he had decorated the summer before. He was put into Philip's old bedroom, with nurses to care for him around the clock.

Elena went to Long Island with her brother and sister-in-law, but stayed in her room most of the time. Although her friends Jean-Paul and Christopher were not welcome as far as Lynn was concerned, they kept in touch by phone. When Elena's French ladies' maid, Yvonne, innocently asked Lynn, "Will Mr. Jean-Paul and Mr. Christopher be coming to visit, Mrs. Manziano?" Lynn screamed at her, "Those two will never step foot in this house again!"

While Angelo slept most of the time, Lynn's behavior became more and more bizarre. She took to hiding bottles of vodka in Elena's bedroom and coming in several times a day, insisting that Elena join in her alcoholic indulgence. Elena, who was no longer in any condition to drink that much liquor, dreaded the hours she was forced to spend every day watching Lynn boozing it up.

When Jean-Paul called Elena, she would whisper, "I would not have suspected it before, but Lynn is a real alcoholic. I never knew it because she has a very high tolerance, and up till now she has always been very cagey about her drinking. Now she no longer cares if I know, because she wants a drinking buddy. I don't know how much more of this I can take. Oh, and another thing, she refuses to let Mother know that Angelo is dying. She says that Mother will interfere, so she keeps on telling her that he has hepatitis but will soon be fine. Under no circumstances will she let her come and visit her son. If I try to give her advice, she becomes hysterical. Oh my God, here she comes again. I'd better get off the phone or she'll question me for hours."

"Okay, but call if you need us. Anytime, day or night. 'Bye."

"Who was that on the phone, Elena?"

"I was just making sure what time Dan would be coming out from the city to do my hair tomorrow. He still has a hard time understanding me. What I hate is when people pretend that they understand what I'm saying and I know that they don't. That drives me crazy."

By this time Lynn had the bottle of vodka out of the closet and was paying little attention to Elena's problems with her speech.

"How's Angelo doing today?" asked Elena.

"I have enough ice in the glass for the two of us, but where in hell did we put the tonic? Oh well, we don't really need it anyway. You know, it's costing a fortune to have Dan still do your hair and makeup everyday. You really should try and do it yourself or have Yvonne help you."

Lynn completely ignored the fact that, although Elena had always done her own hair and makeup before the injury to her brain, she now had lost the ability to do many of the things she had always taken for granted.

Elena knew that the best course of action was to say nothing and pretend to sip her drink. She didn't want to further irritate the irascible Lynn. After all, her husband was dying in the next room.

—

As the summer wore on, Maria became more and more alarmed that she was no longer able to speak to her son, who did not seem to be getting any better.

By August Maria was frantic with worry. "Lynn, honey, don't you think that Angelo should see another doctor? I don't think that this one is doing much good."

"I really can't put up with your complaints anymore. He's getting the best of care. That's all that matters."

"Well then, could I say 'Hello' to my Elena, please?"

"Sorry, but your Elena is having her hair done again and can't come to the phone."

"Then please, honey, give her my love. And also to my boy."

By then, Maria was talking to herself. She hadn't realized that the click she had heard was Lynn's way of terminating the conversation.

That same afternoon, one of the nurses knocked on the door of Elena's bedroom to tell her that Angelo's vital organs had failed. When Elena went to Lynn's room to give her the news, she found her sister-in-law in a deep alcoholic sleep on the bed, snoring loudly. Knowing that there was nothing she could do to rouse her brother's wife, Elena went to Angelo's bedside and held his hand until he peacefully passed away.

When Lynn finally woke up, there was another outburst of hysteria, then more vodka before she called Carlo and told him that he was the one who had to tell "the old lady" that her son was dead. Carlo and his wife Bea were on the next flight from California to New York to break the news to his mother, and were already preparing to implement their own plans, picking up where Angelo and Lynn had left off. They expected Lynn to be child's play to deal with, now that her husband was gone.

～

When Angelo was laid out for viewing at the funeral home, Jean-Paul felt that he had to make an appearance, no matter how much Lynn resented him. He was "damned if he did and damned if he didn't," so he went.

Lynn thought it best to have a closed casket, since her husband had lost more than fifty pounds during his illness. When Jean-Paul arrived, the only person present was Lynn, who greeted him with the good manners that the occasion required.

He kissed her cheek and said, "I'm so sorry, Lynn."

He could smell the vodka as she answered through gritted teeth, "Jean-Paul, how sweet of you to come."

"Of course I came. The three of us shared many wonderful memories over the years. I can never forget that."

Jean-Paul could tell that her husband's death had not softened her attitude towards him. She still perceived Jean-Paul as the enemy. It was an awkward moment for both of them, and Jean-Paul quickly went and stood in front of the casket for a few moments, pretending to be in prayerful meditation for the deceased. But what he was really thinking was, I have nothing to say to this woman who hates me because of her late husband's jealousy and lies. How the hell do I get out of here gracefully? Oh shit, I hear Nana's voice. She must be arriving with Carlo and Bea. I'd better make a quick exit. At least they'll all know that I came to pay my respects.

Maria waddled in, looking fragile but stoic, and hardly seemed to notice when Jean-Paul gave her the obligatory kiss on the cheek with his condolences.

It was Carlo and Bea who surprised him with their friendly greeting. He barely knew them, but he couldn't help thinking, I wonder what these two are up to now, and if they expect to take over Elena's affairs. He had seen enough of the family's greed not to be suspicious of everyone's motives. At least Carlo was a doctor, with an apparently good practice in California.

Jean-Paul asked them, "Is Elena coming?"

"We're bringing her over later," Bea answered a little too quickly.

By this time Jean-Paul was more than ready to say his goodbyes to the family. Lynn, however, had disappeared from the room.

On his way out of the funeral home, Jean-Paul saw Lynn, popping a breath mint into her mouth as she was leaving the ladies' room. It was the first time he had ever seen her unsteady on her feet.

He thought, She must have a flask stashed in her handbag to help her cope with the Manzianos.

After all, Lynn was an intelligent woman, and she knew that with Angelo gone, she no longer had any standing in the family. As far as Maria, Carlo, and Bea were concerned, she was as dead as her husband.

CHAPTER 15

As soon as they had arrived in New York City, Carlo and Bea had installed themselves in the large sitting room at the front of Elena's apartment—the room off the foyer, nearest the front door, where they could keep tabs on all the people coming or going. They removed the Louis XVI settee from underneath an enormous painting by Gauguin, and replaced it with a bed.

Carlo confided to Elena, "You know, this is the first time that Bea has left the house in California in three years. She has stayed home and lived on barbiturates by day and gin martinis at night." Jean-Paul was convinced that it could only be Carlo himself who had prescribed the drugs for her.

Carlo and Bea often went home to California, and Jean-Paul prayed that it was not to prepare themselves to come and live with Elena in New York City.

When Jean-Paul was not working, he and Christopher still came and had dinner with Elena. But they noticed that something was different. Things were not the same when Carlo and Bea were there. There was an atmosphere one couldn't quite explain, but everyone was on guard.

Jean-Paul and Christopher were out shopping with Elena one afternoon, when she said, "After Philip died, Angelo wanted me to make out a will leaving him, rather than Angelina and my grandchild, the bulk of my estate. He and Lynn were to inherit the majority, with only a small portion going to Angelina. But he died before it could be written up. Now Carlo and Bea want me to make out a will making them the main beneficiaries of my estate, leaving Angelina and Gregorio out in the cold again."

～

It wasn't long before Carlo and Bea placed a new will in front of Elena and said, "With Angelo gone, we'll take care of you now. Therefore we need you to sign this new will, so we can stay here and take care of you. It says that when you die you leave two-thirds of your estate to us, part of it to your mother, and the rest to Angelina. This way you will never be left alone to fend for yourself."

In other words, "Now that your husband is dead and Angelo is dead and you have a motor disability, you had better sign this document or we'll leave you alone in the world. You know that no one will take better care of you than your family—and we are it! Turn us down and you'll have no one."

Elena played along with her brother and sister-in-law, and signed the will they presented to her. As soon as they had left the room, she called Jean-Paul and told him what had just occurred.

She then said, "Jean-Paul, darling, I need a lawyer right away to make out a new will that will be according to my wishes and not theirs. Do you know of someone we can trust who can help us?"

"Just give me a few minutes and I'll have an answer for you."

"All right, but call back on my private phone. Carlo and Bea have a habit of listening in on the other one."

"No problem. This won't take long."

The one person he trusted more than any other to help Elena in her dilemma was Helen Dawson, the Broadway and film star with whom he had become great friends ever since they had done a television show together a few years before. As with Elena, there had been an instant rapport between the two of them, which had evolved into daily phone calls from wherever they were in the world.

She was one of the few great stars who were beloved by all the many people who work together to make a Broadway show a success. The first thing Jean-Paul had said to the iconic star when they had met backstage before the taping of the television show was, "One of the most exciting nights of my life was when Philip and Elena Zimmerman gave me and their daughter, Angelina, tickets to the opening night of your movie The Five Donohues in 1954. Not only was it was our first date, but it was also the first time I saw you in person, when you arrived at the theater and sat a few seats away from us. It was quite a thrill for a young fan!"

"Come on back to my dressing room after the show. We can go someplace and celebrate. You are old enough to drink, aren't you, kid? You know, the Zimmermans introduced me to my third husband. That was a marriage I could have phoned in. Oops! See you later. I think I hear my cue."

It was always difficult for a legendary star to trust many people. But Helen's instincts, like Elena's, were right on target with this young man. In return, he understood immediately that not only could they trust him, but also that they would always be there for him.

After promising Elena that he would find a way to solve the predicament of the wills, he dialed Helen's number. "Hi, Helen, it's me. Elena Zimmerman's brother and sister-in-law just made her sign a will giving them most of her assets, and her daughter and grandson a pittance. She needs the name of a lawyer she can trust who can make out another will that her family won't know about."

"Honey, Harry Haimoff can do anything Elena wants, and do it her way. Let me call him on the other phone right now. Hang on and I'll see if he can make time today. If Elena gets hit by a truck in the next twenty-four hours, then her daughter and grandson will be screwed. Hold on.

"Hello Harry, this is Helen. Can you see a friend of mine this afternoon? It's important or I wouldn't ask. She needs a new will to make the one her family made her sign this morning invalid. And the family need never know about it! The name's Zimmerman, but keep it under your hat. She'll be coming with a young friend of mine. Okay, two-thirty it is. Thanks for everything. 'Bye Harry! Love to the family!"

Jean-Paul was ecstatic and cried, "Oh, Helen, that's great. Thanks a million. I'll call you later."

That afternoon Elena and Jean-Paul went to the offices of Harry Haimoff. Elena asked Jean-Paul to stay with her, in case the lawyer had difficulty understanding her speech.

Elena's new will stated that the majority of her estate, including the Zimmerman Trust, would go to her daughter, Angelina. There were also a few generous bequests to friends such as Dan, who had been her hairdresser and makeup man over the years. As for Carlo and Bea, they were taken care of, but not nearly in the way they had expected. Afterwards, Jean-Paul escorted a beaming Elena back home in time for a celebratory cocktail.

〜

Harry Haimoff prepared Elena's will that afternoon. The next day, after she had signed the will in his office, she and Jean-Paul went back to her apartment and taped a copy under her dressing table. Only Elena, Jean-Paul, Christopher, Angelina, and Gregorio knew about the hidden document. Carlo and Bea continued to live in a state of blissful ignorance, believing that once Elena died they would be rich beyond their wildest imaginings. The fact that they were older than she and had no children of their own never entered their minds. It was as though they believed that they would live forever.

Now that Carlo and Bea felt secure in the illusion that they were the major inheritors of Elena's will, Carlo presented Elena with their next demand: "Bea and I feel that you are entitled to ask your lawyer to take action against Lynn for the return of the five hundred thousand dollars you gave to Angelo, plus the apartment and the diamond box."

Even Elena was angry that Lynn wanted to keep the diamond box, which Angelo had plainly asked for as a loan. But for once she stood up to the pair and said, "I gave the apartment to Angelo outright. Then Lynn inherited it from her husband. The five hundred thousand was also a gift. There's no way we can take that back. However, the diamond box, which is worth about five hundred thousand dollars, was on loan, and I would like to have it back, since it was a gift to me from Philip."

The greedy couple still wanted it all, but in the end the lawyers agreed with Elena, and only sued Lynn for the return of the diamond box.

"You see, Elena, we were right all along about Lynn. We don't think she should be in our lives after the lawsuit we had to go through to make her return your property," crowed Bea, who was obviously the leader of the pack when it came to her and Carlo. "We don't think she should be welcome in our—your—home anymore."

The two were still traveling back and forth from California, preparing for the day when they would return on a permanent basis.

In the meantime, Bea was slowly trying to morph into Elena.

Elena told Jean-Paul, "Bea's behavior is becoming more and more bizarre. My maid told me this morning that Bea goes into my bathroom and takes the pantyhose that I throw away in the wastebasket. Now what would she want with my old pantyhose?"

Elena did not know that her sister-in-law had also walked into Bergdorf's with the store's charge card, which she had taken from Elena's wallet, and had told the saleslady, "I'm Mrs. Zimmerman. Would you please charge these things to my account? Here's my card."

Bea knew that Elena would never find out, because Carlo never showed his sister the bills. He wrote the checks for Elena to sign and, because she trusted him, she never checked the charges.

And that was just the beginning. Whenever she could, Bea became Elena Zimmerman. She adored the feeling of power it gave her when people bowed and scraped in front of the Zimmerman name. She had no idea that on her, the hair, the makeup and the clothes were a poor imitation of Elena.

—

Ironically, it was on the first floor at Bergdorf's that Jean-Paul and Christopher ran into Lynn. As soon as Lynn saw them, she burst into tears.

"Oh, I can't believe it. I've missed you both so much. Why don't we go down the street and have a drink?"

"Sure, Lynn, we'd love to," said the two men in unison. But what they were really thinking was, I wonder what she wants from us!

Once they were seated with three Bloody Marys in front of them, Lynn finally dried her tears and said, "I never understood why you didn't come to Long Island to visit us when Angelo was dying. I kept waiting to hear from you, but you never called."

"But Lynn," answered Jean-Paul, "we heard that, as far as you and Angelo were concerned, we were not welcome at the house."

"Whoever told you such a stupid thing is lying. It's probably Carlo and Bea trying to make more trouble. None of it is true. You know how much Angelo and I always cared for you."

She then became coy and said in simpering tones, "I want you to know that I'm seeing someone now. His name is Bobbie Lane and he's a forty-year-old stockbroker. He made love to me the first night we met. Angelo couldn't make love to me during the last years we were married, when he was so sick. And believe me, I'm making up for lost time."

The real reason for Lynn's newfound camaraderie became evident when she said too casually, "By the way, how is Elena? I'd love to see her again. Do you think that you could arrange for us to meet sometime for dinner when Carlo and Bea are away? I miss her so much."

They knew that Lynn would be counting on Elena's innate generosity if they met, and would try to manipulate something out of her—maybe even the box covered in diamonds that had been returned by court order to the vitrine in Elena's apartment.

"We'll see what we can do. But we can't promise you anything. All we can do is try," answered Jean-Paul, who had no intention of getting involved in that can of worms.

Lynn finally got up and said goodbye, with hugs, kisses and vows of eternal love.

"Whew," said Jean-Paul once she had gone. "I can't believe how stupid she must think we are. After refusing to let us come out to Long Island, and then a lawsuit with Elena over the diamond box, she thinks she can come prancing back into all our lives as though nothing ever happened. She must be pretty desperate right now—but at least she's getting laid."

That night, Carlo and Bea were back in California, so Jean-Paul and Christopher told Elena about their encounter with Lynn.

"Please, I've suffered enough because of that woman. I feel sorry for her. I know what loss can be like, but she's put me through a lot since Angelo died. You know how embarrassing it was for me, with my unintelligible speech, to be called up in a courtroom to testify about the diamond box. I'll never get over the humiliation of that day. It would almost have been worth giving it to her with all the rest."

Lynn called Jean-Paul a couple of times after their meeting at Bergdorf's. Finally he told her, "For God sakes, Lynn, forget about the past. Go out and live your own life. You're a beautiful woman who can find a wonderful man to marry. How about Mr. Lane? He sounds like a good candidate. And invite me to the wedding. I'll be there to cheer you on!"

Within a few months Lynn did marry her Mr. Lane, and, no, she did not invite Jean-Paul. He found out about it from one of the doormen who worked in Elena's building, who said, "Did you know that Mrs. Manziano has remarried and is now Mrs. Lane? I just heard about it from the doorman in her husband's building. She's selling her apartment and moving in with her new husband."

Jean-Paul only hoped that she had joined AA or some similar organization.

———

When summer came, Elena called Jean-Paul and said, "Why don't you and Christopher come out and spend some time with me in Long Island? I know that you have some time off from work and it seems like an ideal place for us to relax and have a good time together. Carlo and Bea are not scheduled to come back for a couple of weeks."

The two weeks were idyllic. There was never a moment of tension. The three of them loved each other's company and laughter was the order of the day.

But when Carlo and Bea came back to the East Coast and joined them on Long Island, it took less than twenty-four hours for all hell to break loose. The three friends were not prepared for the negative energy these two people brought with them.

The unpleasantness started on the first morning after Carlo and Bea arrived. When Bea walked into the dining room where Jean-Paul and Christopher were having a leisurely breakfast, the two young men smiled and said, "Good morning, Bea. How are you today?"

She sat down at the place that had been set for her, and without warning, she swept her silverware, napkin, and coffee cup off the table and onto the floor, stood back up, and screamed, "You all hate me, and if that is the case, Carlo and I will pack up and leave immediately."

"Wha-what did we do, Bea? We don't understand."

Before they could say any more, she had stormed upstairs to her room in tears. Jean-Paul and Christopher were stunned at Bea's unexpected performance and had no idea what had brought this tantrum on.

They gave her some time to calm down before they cornered Carlo in the kitchen. He was fixing a tray with coffee and toast for his wife.

"Carlo, what on earth happened? What is Bea so upset about? We've been nice to her ever since you both arrived. Can we go upstairs and talk with her?"

Carlo, who was not the bravest soul in the world, said, "I suppose you could. I really don't know what's the matter with her either."

They followed Carlo upstairs, where Bea was lying prostrate on the bed in what had once been Philip's bedroom, and was also the room in which Angelo had died.

The young men tried to appease her for Elena's sake. "Bea, we don't understand the problem. Nobody here hates you. In fact, we were all happy to see you arrive last night."

By late afternoon there was a semblance of peace, after everyone assured and reassured Bea that she was the greatest thing ever to have arrived in Long Island. Now they understood that not only was she a neurotic, high-maintenance woman with a weak husband, but also one who had a very specific agenda—an agenda that was not going to be in Elena's best interest.

It did not take long for the woman's true nature to become very clear to Jean-Paul and Christopher. In essence it was Angelo and Lynn all over again—only worse. An atmosphere of pure evil had entered the house.

Elena had recently hired a sweet young maid who was, as far as anyone could see, a cheerful and willing worker. The two young men were on the porch talking to Bea when the smiling maid walked by on her way to the kitchen. The moment the maid left the room, a wicked look came across Bea's face as she snarled, "I'll soon wipe the smile off of her face."

—

With Bea's wildly fluctuating behavior dominating the house, Elena was as miserable as Jean-Paul and Christopher were. Finally Christopher went into Elena's room and told her bluntly, "Elena, if you're not happy with your brother and his wife in the house, you shouldn't have to put up with the situation. Remember, you hold all the cards."

"But he's my brother. I can't throw him out of my house. He also takes care of my business and pays all the bills. All I have to do is sign the checks. Carlo is family, and you can't desert family. Look at me, I can't even make myself understood when I speak. I can't take the chance of being alone."

"Okay, then, why don't you come with Jean-Paul and me when we start touring next month? We'll be in British Columbia for a while, and maybe afterwards we can vacation in Hawaii for ten days, like we did before."

"I can't believe it. You're saving my life again. We'll leave those two behind and have a ball, like old times. Yes! Let's go."

———

The next three years were wonderful, as long as the three were traveling. Elena was a great sport about any and every inconvenience, even spending a whole night sitting in an airport in New Mexico because their flight to Acapulco had been canceled at the last minute.

The three of them got a two-bedroom suite in every hotel they stayed in—one bedroom for Elena, one for Jean-Paul and Christopher, and a living room in between. They had a silly little machine that laughed when it was turned on. The first one up in the morning would put the machine outside the other bedroom door and turn it on. Whoever was still in bed would hear the contraption laughing away, and knew that it was about time to get up and order breakfast.

The only time this little gag backfired was when they arrived in Canada and the surly customs man took one look at the twenty or so suitcases they traveled with. Elena had put the laughing machine inside a small Louis

Vuitton suitcase that held her jewelry. When the agent picked up the small bag, he asked, "What's in this?"

"That's Mrs. Zimmerman's jewelry."

For some inexplicable reason, the agent tried to shake it. In doing so he managed to somehow turn on the laughing machine that Elena had put inside the case at the last minute. The man became apoplectic when all of customs suddenly heard this insane laughter coming from the bag he held in his hands. Of course, Elena, Jean-Paul, and Christopher did their best to control their own laughter.

The customs agent was not amused, but let the three loonies leave anyway, while he still had some semblance of dignity left.

That's the way it was wherever they went. They were like three kids laughing their way around the world, while Carlo and Bea were stewing in Elena's vast apartment, thinking of ways to get her back under their control. They had plans that did not include Jean-Paul and Christopher, but were smart enough not to make any waves yet, as far as Elena's two young friends were concerned.

—

In 1975 Jean-Paul and Christopher went to Los Angeles for a television series that might keep them out on the West Coast for a long time. Elena stayed behind in New York with Carlo and Bea, but within two days she called the boys.

"Jean-Paul, what do you think of my coming out for a couple of weeks to visit?"

"Of course, Elena, that would be great. You can stay with us in the house we just rented in Beverly Hills. It's too big for just the two of us anyway, and has a beautiful view."

Within two days Elena had joined them.

⁓

For Elena's conniving brother and sister-in-law, having Elena stay in California with her young men was bad enough, but the fact that Angelina, Mark, and their son Gregorio lived in nearby San Marino was too much of a threat for them to bear. After nine months elapsed, Elena received word that Carlo and Bea were coming to visit them in Beverly Hills.

The "visit" was not something that any of them looked forward to, but since the house had a guest cottage near the swimming pool, they knew that the Manzianos would have their own quarters.

The first few days passed without too much drama from Bea. Therefore Jean-Paul and Christopher were surprised when Elena went to them and said regretfully, "Carlo has told me that I must return to New York because my money is being rapidly depleted by my lifestyle, even though we share the cost of the house. I hate to go, but right now I have no choice."

Jean-Paul and Christopher knew that she was still a very wealthy woman. It was inconceivable to them that a fearless woman like Elena would allow her family to manipulate her in such a brutish manner. But they could also see that Elena was so overwhelmed by the ridiculous fear of poverty that her trusted brothers had instilled in her, that she now felt powerless to do anything but quietly acquiesce to their demands.

Elena had been brought up by Maria, and all her life she had been taught to believe that her family was the most important responsibility she would ever have. As her mother had repeatedly emphasized, "Why else would God have made you so beautiful!" That belief, coupled with the damage to the motor portion of her brain, had made her, for the first time in her life, afraid of being alone and unable to fend for herself.

Elena had no idea of the price she would pay for her unyielding loyalty to her family.

CHAPTER 16

As the years went by, Elena went out less and less. Jean-Paul and Christopher were still living in California, and without Jean-Paul's loving arm to hold on to, she seldom left her apartment in Manhattan.

In order to keep Elena close to home when her "boys" came to town, and to prevent her from going back to California with them, Bea would put on a tragic face and say, "Oh, Elena, I don't know how to tell you this, but we just found out that Carlo has a serious heart condition and may not live much longer. I'm so sorry to have to break this news to you. I don't know what we'll do without him. But don't worry, I'll be here for you."

After a year or so, when Carlo still looked as healthy as a bull, Bea changed her tune. Suddenly Carlo's heart condition was forgotten and she was the one with the terminal illness.

Bea sent Carlo into Elena's bedroom to say, "I'm devastated to have to tell you this, but Bea has a serious melanoma and the doctors don't give her much of a chance for survival. All we can do right now is support her as much as we can."

Cancer would become Bea's disease of choice. It was something that could go on indefinitely while everyone held their breath wondering whether she was going to survive or not. The stories of fatal diseases went back and forth over time, according to how threatened Bea and Carlo felt at the prospect of Elena's leaving again. The two of them were taking no chances of someone else's replacing them and living off the "fat of the land."

At first Elena's natural compassion kept her in line, but after a while their stories began to grow old. She eventually learned to make the appropriate sympathetic sounds, while inwardly rolling her eyes in disbelief. She was on to them, but played along in order to keep peace in the house.

⁓

By 1980, to Carlo and Bea's dismay, Elena still had her hairdresser and makeup man, Dan, come to the house every day—something else that they felt was taking the bread out of their mouths. Dan, his assistant Sheila, and the manicurist kept Elena company for at least a part of the day. It was one of the few pleasures she had left.

In California, the boys had always seen to it that she had someone come to the house on a daily basis to make her pretty. And when they traveled, Jean-Paul had discovered that he was quite gifted at doing her hair, while Christopher was in charge of her eyelashes. Between their efforts and Elena's natural beauty, she still stopped traffic.

Dan kept Elena as a daily client in New York, but he had gone on to get his real estate license, and had been doing quite well on a free-lance basis.

One day, while sitting in her makeup chair, Elena had a brainstorm. "Dan, wouldn't it be nice if I could find a lovely apartment with a beautiful terrace overlooking

Central Park? Philip certainly left me enough furniture and art to furnish it. What do you think?"

Dan was in hog heaven at the thought of the commission he would get, both from selling the eighteen-room Zimmerman apartment and then buying a new, lavish one for Elena to live in. That kind of double deal would be any real estate broker's dream.

Dan was nearly salivating at the thought as he said, "Oh, Mrs. Zimmerman, that's a wonderful idea. I'll get right on it today. I know just the kind of apartment you would love. You can trust me!"

It turned out that Dan was as good at selling apartments as he was with hair and makeup. The first place he showed her was perfection. It was on Fifth Avenue, with a view of Central Park, where she could sit on a terrace and look out at the trees and talk to Philip, asking for his protection. She felt that his spirit would protect her now the way he had always tried to do in life.

The apartment was in a magnificent old building and had already been decorated with beautiful boiserie in the library and stunning fabrics on the walls—a perfect complement to her artwork. It was a large apartment, a whole floor, although not quite as large as the eighteen-room apartment she was selling.

"Elena," said Carlo, with Bea close by his side, "now that you have found a new apartment, if you wish to buy it and decorate it the way you want, you will have to sell your thirty-carat blue-white diamond ring back to Harry Winston. You have not got the means to continue your extravagant lifestyle without making certain sacrifices. We can always have a good copy made for you to wear."

Jean-Paul was shocked when he heard that Carlo and Bea were insisting that Elena sell the ring because she was broke. Again, what they were telling Elena made no sense. She had quite enough money to do as she pleased. And the Manzianos themselves had no problem in taking a salary of $25,000 per month to "manage" the Widow Zimmerman's affairs. "Elena, that was the only piece of jewelry that really meant something to you. You wore it on the fourth finger of your left hand whether we were swimming in the Caribbean Sea, or dressed to the nines at the 'April in Paris' ball in New York City."

"I can't help it, Jean-Paul, Carlo says that it has to go if I want to buy the apartment. He says I have no choice since there is very little money left. Anyway, you're going to love the apartment! I can't wait for you two to see it all done, the next time you're in town."

To Jean-Paul's question, "Are you sure you're all right?" Elena gave her usual answer, "I'm great!"

But Jean-Paul knew that for Elena the ring had been a symbol of her eternal beauty and the fulfillment of the accomplishments that her family had expected of her. A copy, as good as it might be, was still a copy, and not the one Philip had given to his bride. Jean-Paul thought it highly probable that Bea's petty and cruel jealousy of Elena's beauty and position in the world had prompted her husband's urging the sale of the precious item, while Carlo took a hefty commission for himself—a commission that Elena let him have because, as she told Jean-Paul, "It will keep him honest."

―

Elena was in her element working with the decorators, fixing up two bedrooms for herself. One was to be used as a bedroom and the other was outfitted as a dressing room with mirrored closets on two walls. It was set up for her to sit like a queen while Dan did her hair and makeup. It also contained the dressing table that had her new will taped under the center drawer.

Carlo and Bea were not unhappy with their suite, which contained a sitting room/office, a bedroom and two bathrooms. Their whole area was self-contained, with a door leading into a small foyer, which opened onto their rooms. Therefore the Manzianos' rooms could be closed off from the rest of the apartment. This was an arrangement that particularly pleased Bea.

When they had all moved in, Carlo and Bea went all out with their program to persuade Elena that she was poor, and did their best to begin isolating her from the rest of the world.

Since Elena no longer had the same social life she had had with Philip or with Jean-Paul and Christopher in California, she had put most of her jewelry collection in a safety deposit box at the bank. Then, whenever Carlo and Bea denied her something she wanted, or she wanted to help someone she knew, she asked Dan to go to Harry Winston or Van Cleef & Arpels and sell a piece she no longer used. Of course, Dan kept a hefty commission for himself.

As the box became more depleted, she put a letter inside, with Carlo's name on it. In the event of her death she wanted him to know why the safety deposit box was empty, or nearly so.

⸺

Decorating had always been something that Elena enjoyed doing, a way to express her artistic side, and she had been content decorating the new apartment. It kept her busy for a while, but when it was over, she found herself once again spending days alone in her room with just the television for company.

When her boys, Jean-Paul and Christopher, flew into town, the three of them would go out every night. This was something that Carlo and Bea just had to accept—that was one connection that they had no control over.

Since Jean-Paul also wanted to see his friend, the show business legend Helen Dawson, who lived in New York, he often asked her to join them. Soon Elena's phone started ringing when the young men were gone.

Helen understood Elena's lonely plight and would often call and say, "Elena, it's Helen, how about going to dinner with me and some of my friends tonight? I know the boys are out of town, but my friend Morty, you remember Morty, the tall, blonde handsome guy—gay as a goose, but a sweetheart—will pick you up at seven o'clock and bring you to my house for a drink before we go to dinner. How does that sound?"

"I'd love to, Helen. Thank you for thinking of me. I'll be ready at seven."

"That's great. We'll see you later. 'Bye, Elena!"

One of the wonderful things about Helen Dawson was her compassion and loyalty to her friends. She felt deeply about Elena's condition and remembered the beautiful and vital woman she had first met years before. The brassy performer had a heart as big as her voice, and she was determined to do anything she could do to bring some joy into Elena's world—a world which, thanks to Carlo and Bea, was constantly shrinking.

Then came the day the conniving couple dreaded the most: Jean-Paul called Elena and said, "Guess what! We're moving back to New York, because I've been offered a year's engagement at a club in the city. I only do one show a night from Monday through Thursday and two on Friday and Saturday. We'll be flying back next Tuesday, and expect to see you that night."

"Oh, Jean-Paul, nothing could make me happier. Give my love to Christopher."

Needless to say, opening night was a huge success, with Helen Dawson taking over a table of ten. One of her guests was Elena, who wore a black velvet Valentino evening gown with a satin ruffle that went around her neck all the way down to her décolletage. Her now-blonde hair had been carefully coiffed by Dan to frame her still lovely face.

From that day forward, the two women were in the audience at least twice a week. Helen brought every friend she knew, while Elena always walked in on Christopher's arm. It was quite a tribute to Jean-Paul to have such a distinguished and loyal following.

Elena had now passed her sixtieth birthday, but everyone she met was still in awe of her beauty and charisma. And her sense of humor remained intact.

By 1984, Carlo and Bea were at their wits' end, wondering how much longer they would have to wait for Elena to die so they could inherit her estate. Then an unexpected ray of light came into their lives—Jean-Paul was offered work in London and Paris, and they would have Elena all to themselves, with no interference.

—

After Jean-Paul and Christopher went to Europe, Carlo and Bea began taking away the few enjoyments Elena had left in her life. First, they started firing the servants—especially those who had demonstrated allegiance to Elena. When it came down to it, they were not shy about telling her, "Either the maid you love so much goes, or we go!"

Her faithful cook, Nora, was one of the first to go. She had come to the Zimmerman house as a seventeen-year-old kitchen helper who did the dirty work that was below the head chef's dignity. She had stayed on for decades, and was promoted to head cook when Philip became ill. Her devotion to and admiration for Elena had been unwavering over the years.

Nora may have been tiny—at least a foot and a half shorter than Bea—but she feared no one and had an indomitable spirit. Otherwise she would not have survived Carlo and Bea's constant harassment.

"Nora," said Bea in her haughtiest tone of voice, "Mrs. Zimmerman can no longer afford to keep you on. Your services will no longer be required. We hope you can arrange to leave as soon as possible."

"But, Mrs. Manziano, who will cook Mrs. Zimmerman's meals when I'm gone?"

"That's not your problem," replied a curt Bea. "And don't bother Mrs. Zimmerman about this. We think it best for you to leave quietly."

Tears welled up in Nora's eyes as she looked at the woman who was so coldly dismissing her. The last words she ever spoke to Bea in her lilting Irish brogue were, "God help Mrs. Zimmerman. You're a cold woman, Mrs. Manziano."

Of course, Nora never received any severance pay, not even a "Thank you for your years of service."

That night Carlo went into Elena's bedroom and said, "Now that Nora is gone, I'm going to cook dinner for Bea and myself. You can order yours from the coffee shop on Madison Avenue."

By then, there was only one maid, Veronica, to do all the work in the big apartment. Most of the time she would be doing chores for Bea. Sometimes, when it was snowing or raining, Bea would send her out to shop for one item at the grocery store several blocks away. When she returned, Bea would think of another item for the poor woman to get at the same store. If the weather was really bad, Bea would keep up this sadistic routine until the maid was thoroughly cold and soaking wet, with tears streaming down her face.

Carlo and Bea evidently had decided, since Elena refused to make them rich by dying, that they would have to convince her of her dire state of poverty; then, one piece at a time, they could sell the priceless works of art that Elena, unbeknownst to them, had willed to a museum, and pocket the proceeds for themselves. The legal and moral issues surrounding their tactics didn't bother them in the least.

But just when Carlo and Bea thought they had the playing field to themselves, another interloper entered the scene.

Gregorio, Angelina's son, was coming to New York to join a public relations firm that had snapped him up as soon as he graduated from college. He was bright, handsome, and had inherited much of his grandmother's humor and generosity of spirit.

Angelina called Elena on her private line and said, "Mummy, Gregorio is going to New York for a wonderful job offer, and wonders if it would be all right if he stayed with you at the apartment until he gets his bearings in the Big City. I know that you and he have never known each other very well, but he's a wonderful young man. I'm sure that you two will get along brilliantly."

"I'd love it! When is he coming? He can have whichever guest room he wants. Tell him that this is his home too."

"He'll be flying out this weekend, and should be at your house on Saturday afternoon."

"Great! I'll be ready for him. But when are you coming to visit?"

"I don't know, Mummy. I don't want to sound like Carlo and Bea, but my husband, Mark, has not been well lately and is going back into the hospital for more tests next week. They say that he has a disease called lupus, and the only medication that they have been giving him is cortisone. I'll be out to see you as soon as I feel that his condition is stabilized."

"Don't you worry about me, Angelina, just take good care of your husband and I'll take care of your son. We'll call you as soon as he arrives. 'Bye."

"'Bye, Mummy, and thanks for everything."

That Saturday, Bea stayed in her room, while Carlo did his best to give the boy a civil greeting. As soon as Carlo went back to his quarters, Elena showed Gregorio his room and bath. The young man wasn't sure how he would get on with the grandmother he had never really known; for most of his life, they had lived three thousand miles away from each other.

Angelina's son endeared himself immediately to Elena when he suggested that they open a bottle of champagne to celebrate their reunion. Of course, Carlo had banned his sister's favorite drink from the house because it was too expensive. But when Elena wanted to give Gregorio the money to go out and buy a bottle of Dom Perignon at the liquor store, the boy refused and said, "Sorry, Lolo, but I'm buying tonight. And we can order dinner in and have it together in your room."

Elena, who after all those lonely nights thought she had died and gone to heaven, burst out with, "Gregorio, I knew you'd bring some joy into this house today. Let's celebrate."

And it was that way every night. Lonely dinners were a thing of the past. Gregorio and Elena talked and laughed while they ate on trays that he would set up every night in her bedroom. They discovered the magic of kindred spirits. Those evenings with his grandmother were a gift that Gregorio would remember for the rest of his life.

The only ones suffering were Carlo and Bea.

"Carlo, you have to get that boy out of here! He's ruining everything. How many years do you think I want to wait until we have what we came here for? I'm telling you for the last time to get that boy out of here. I don't care how you do it."

"But, Bea," said Carlo, with the silly little giggle that came out whenever he was unsure of himself, "there's nothing I can do right now. He's young and will soon move on with his life. You could at least get out of your bathrobe once in a while, comb your hair, and make an appearance. It's hard for me to keep saying that you're too sick to come out of your room."

"Well, where are those pills you promised me yesterday? I'm almost out of the last prescription. And you know that I won't be happy at all if they're not here by the time I run out of them! Oh yes, and one more thing. That fat, useless mother of yours, Maria, who has spent the last twenty years of her life rocking back and forth on that stinking old couch of hers, had better not use up any more of Elena's money. Now that the old woman is in the hospital she might as well die for all the good she is to anyone. And a private room no less—a room your sister insisted upon—is costing us a fortune. Someone should put her out of her misery."

"But, Bea," said Carlo with another little giggle, "I didn't want to tell you before speaking to Elena first, but Mother died this morning. Her heart gave out during the night."

"Ding dong, the witch is dead! It's about time. I hope that pathetic husband of hers doesn't expect to be taken care of for the rest of his life."

"I assume he'll go back to Endicott, where he has family. He's ninety-two years old, you know."

Bea's "kindly" reaction was, "Good!"

⌒

Bea didn't have to worry about going to the funeral. Maria's husband insisted on having it in Endicott, where they had first met. He was grief-stricken. He had really loved his wife and still thought of her as the pretty young girl he had seen arrive in America, with the baby Carlo in her arms and her husband Ernesto at her side.

Elena had inherited Maria's ability to block out anything unpleasant, and now she shut out the reality of her mother's death. She and Carlo would go to Endicott for a couple of days, for the funeral service and interment, and afterward she would never speak of it again.

Bea did not attend the funeral. Her reason, as usual, was that she was ill.

Gregorio would have liked to have stayed in Endicott with the rest of his family, but he had to return to town the same day to finish an advertising campaign. It was an important assignment that, if it worked out, could mean a big promotion for him in the company.

That night, Gregorio arrived at home feeling tired and hungry after a long and difficult day. As he walked past Elena's room, he saw that the lights were on and someone was rummaging through her dressing room closets. He walked in expecting to see Veronica, the maid, cleaning. But instead he found Bea rummaging through his grandmother's clothes and jewelry. The next thing he noticed was the copy of Elena's thirty-carat diamond ring, on his aunt's finger. All of the closets looked as though they had been ransacked.

"What the hell do you think you're doing, Bea? These are my grandmother's closets. And why are you wearing her ring?"

As usual, Bea went on the offensive. "What do you think you're doing, spying on me like that? I'm doing Elena a favor by putting her things back in order. You know what a terrible housekeeper Veronica is. As for the ring, I found it thrown in a drawer over there and put it on my finger so that I wouldn't forget to put it back in her jewelry box. And what makes you think that I want anything of your grandmother's? Everything I own is just as nice as hers, if not better. I don't know why Carlo and I bother to stay here and watch out for her wellbeing. If this is the thanks we get, we can leave as soon as my husband comes back from Endicott. Anyway, our house in California is every bit as nice as this!"

That said, she huffed out of the dressing room, leaving a stunned Gregorio to clean up the mess.

～

Although Gregorio lived in his grandmother's apartment for another year before being transferred to San Francisco, he never spoke of what he had seen that night in Elena's dressing room. He was afraid that it would start a new battle in which Elena would be the one to suffer in the end.

Bea, however, hoped that he would tell everyone. Then she could rant and rave that Gregorio was making up stories in order to discredit her. But he never gave her that opportunity.

When he finally left for San Francisco, it was with sadness at leaving his grandmother, whom he had come to love deeply, and relief at being away from Carlo and Bea—who were now free to wreak havoc on Elena's life.

CHAPTER 17

At first Bea would tell the maid, "Don't bother cleaning Mrs. Zimmerman's room. Come in and do ours now." But as time went on, the doors to the Manzianos' quarters were locked and no one was allowed in, not even to clean. Instead, Bea would think of all kinds of errands for Veronica to do around town. As a result, the apartment became increasingly filthy. Dust was piling up in every corner.

The real reason that no one was allowed in Carlo and Bea's rooms was that Bea was a hoarder, and soon there was no way for anyone to get through the masses of junk that she was accumulating. After awhile, her stuff began to spread into other parts of the apartment, and every room but Elena's was packed with Bea's useless clutter.

Carlo and Bea went into a frenzy the day that Elena told them, "Jean-Paul and Christopher have returned from Europe and are coming to see me tomorrow."

Bea immediately went to Veronica, who had just returned from another wasted trip to the supermarket for a single can of chicken broth, and said, "I can't believe the way you keep this apartment, Veronica. It's a disgrace. I want all of this mess cleaned up by tomorrow. If you don't know what to do with it, just leave it in the guest rooms. And give a once-over to Mrs. Zimmerman's quarters. It's about time you earned your salary. And don't expect to get a bonus at Christmas. Neither you nor the lazy bunch of doormen and elevator men are getting anything more out of us this year. We're not made of money, you know, and you're not taking advantage of us any more. You can leave our rooms alone, but finish the rest of the job, no matter how long it takes."

"But Mrs. Manziano, I have to pick up my children after school today. I can't work that late."

"If you want to feed those brats of yours, you had better get to work right now and stay until the job is done. You can get someone else to pick them up, but I want this stuff out of sight by tomorrow. And don't forget, a once-over in Mrs. Zimmerman's rooms."

~

The next day when Jean-Paul and Christopher stepped out of the elevator and into the foyer outside the front door of Elena's apartment, they gasped in disbelief.

Jean-Paul said, "Can you believe the dust on that console? And everything on it is filthy too. Oh my God, you can't even see yourself in the mirror anymore. Elena must never go out, or she would have insisted that someone dust the place."

Elena had asked Carlo to leave the front door unlocked so Jean-Paul and Christopher could let themselves in. She no longer had a butler or maids to answer the door and was just as happy if her two friends did not have to contend with her brother and sister-in-law.

Christopher opened the door and said, "It's pitch black in here. There's not a light on in the whole place. We'll have to get to Elena's room by Braille!"

When they reached the long hallway, they saw a light in the distance, which they knew came from Elena's room.

"Christopher," whispered Jean-Paul as though he were entering a church, "all the doors are closed. I can't see into any of the rooms. I wonder if the living room is in as bad a condition as the entryway? Come on, let's go down the hall. This is beginning to get spooky."

From the doorway to her room, the two young men could see the back of Elena's blonde hair as she sat in a chair, facing a silent and dark television.

"Elena," said Jean-Paul softly so as not to frighten her, "we're back."

She never turned her head, but said in a weak voice, "Come in."

The two visitors could tell by the subdued sound of her voice that something was very wrong. They came around, kissed her, and said, "How are you?"

Her voice cracked as she said, "I'm fine."

Then Jean-Paul and Christopher noticed a letter and a small package in Elena's lap.

"No, you're not fine. We know you too well, and your usual answer is, 'I'm great!'—whether it's true or not. Please, Elena, if you can't share it with us, you can't share it with anybody. And if something's wrong, you don't need to be alone. We're always here for you. Always."

Silently, she took the letter out of her lap and handed it to Jean-Paul.

"This arrived in the mail this morning. Carlo and Bea open all my mail, especially if it's marked PERSONAL, so they know about it too."

Jean-Paul read it to himself before passing it on to Christopher. Then Elena handed him the box that had also been in her lap.

"Mirella is Lorenzo's wife. I told you about them, the brain-damaged child that they lost and then their departure for Italy. It's been years now and I've tried not to think about it. I somehow always hoped that someday he would be free to come back to me. Now I know that it's too late. He did a noble thing, and now he's gone forever. I always hoped that, however awful things became with Carlo and Bea, my prince, Lorenzo, would someday arrive on his white horse and make everything all right again. At least he went quickly with a massive stroke, and didn't have to linger like Philip did. For Lorenzo it was over in a few moments. There's some comfort in knowing that. I can see why he never deserted Mirella. They were bound by the tragedy of their only child. She must be a great lady to have written this letter to a woman she never met."

Tears came to Christopher's eyes as he read the last paragraph aloud: "I'm sure that Lorenzo would have wanted you to know that he never, even for one day, forgot you, and would want you to have the watch he wore every day of his life. It's a small thing, but it was his. I hope I was able to bring some comfort into his world. He certainly did in mine. He was loyal and kind right to the end. My dear Elena, I know that in his heart, he was always yours."

The letter was simply signed, "Mirella."

The tears flowed down the three friends' faces as Jean-Paul opened the box and brought out a gold watch with a woven gold band. On the clasp were Lorenzo's initials, LFP. This was the first time Elena knew that he had given his son his middle name, Fabrizio.

"Christopher, Jean-Paul, look, it fits my wrist. I can't believe it. I'll wear it always, and when it's my turn to go, I want you two to have it to remember me by."

"It's really beautiful," said Jean-Paul, "but don't you think that we should have some diamonds put around the face of Lorenzo's watch to make it more feminine for you to wear?"

"Oh no! Carlo would die if I went to the expense of putting diamonds on the watch."

"Hogwash," piped in Christopher, "it'll be our gift to you. We'll take it to Helen Dawson's jeweler, Mr. Lichi. He's great."

"You two are too much for me. If it weren't for you, I might have jumped out of that window today."

"Elena, I think you've been sitting around this apartment for too long. Let's all go out to dinner some-where nice."

"But my hair, my makeup. I'm not ready to be seen."

"More hogwash," said Jean-Paul. "You're almost there. I'll just do a little something more with the hair and Christopher can do the dress-up eyelashes. After that, I think the black Valentino you love so much will be perfect on you tonight."

"Come on Elena, let's go into the dressing room and get started on that hair. Oh my God, it doesn't look like Dan's work anymore."

"It's not. Dan moved to San Francisco with his family, and now his assistant, Sheila, does it. Of course, no one can do the magic that Dan did, but then, Carlo says I can only afford to have her come to the house twice a week. She was here this morning, but you should see me the rest of the time. Not a pretty picture!"

"Stop it, Elena, you're more beautiful than ever. Just let Christopher and me put the icing on the cake."

"I can't believe that you two can still make me feel beautiful."

"But you are beautiful. You are!"

After taking Elena home that night, Jean-Paul was still worried about his old friend. He knew her uncanny ability to put a good face on any situation so as not to burden him or Christopher with doom and gloom. Lorenzo's passing was something she would never again cry about in front of them, no matter how much she suffered inside.

~

When Mr. Lichi had put the diamonds around the face of Lorenzo's watch, "the boys," as Elena still called Jean-Paul and Christopher, took it to her. All they said when they opened the box was, "Ta-da!"

Elena clapped her hands and laughed like a little girl, "Oh, thank you so much. I'll wear it every day." She posed for them, moving her wrist back and forth so they could admire the diamonds from every angle. Only her two friends saw the tears in her eyes, gleaming through the smile.

The appalling condition of Elena's apartment was never mentioned among the three friends. But each time the boys asked, "How are Carlo and Bea?" Elena would simply roll her eyes. Period. She wasn't going to complain. If she did, she would have to throw her brother and his wife out of the house and find some other way to take care of her affairs—something she no longer felt capable of doing.

~

It was not long after Lorenzo's death that the boys had to break some more devastating news to Elena—news that was painful for all of them.

They went to the apartment to pick Elena up for dinner. Before leaving for the restaurant, Jean-Paul said, "You know, Elena, the newspapers have had stories in the last week about our friend Helen Dawson missing a performance at the Academy Awards because of illness. The truth is that minutes before she was to leave for Los Angeles, she had a seizure and had to be taken to the hospital. The doctors and nurses were wonderful about protecting her privacy, but the world will soon know that Helen has brain cancer. They tried to operate, but it's too late. It's one of those things that's not evident until it gets too far along to do anything about. How ironic that she had a complete physical a couple of weeks before, and was given a clean bill of health. At that time she complained about some disturbing symptoms, but the doctor told her it was probably caused by stress from all the concert engagements that she had had in the past year. Now she has been told that she has no more than six months to live."

"No, not Helen!" cried Elena. "She was so kind and generous, inviting me out with her friends. I kept meaning to call her and reciprocate, but was afraid because only you two understand my garbled speech. Now it's too late."

At dinner, the boys, who had been at Helen's bedside almost every day, explained the horrific details of the superstar's agony more fully.

"Poor Helen, she can no longer speak and is slowly losing the use of her arms and legs. All she has left is the ability to scream and cry when she wants to express herself. It's almost impossible to believe that this is the same woman who has thrilled audiences for decades with her incredible voice."

Elena listened quietly and then excused herself to go to the ladies' room. Jean-Paul escorted her as usual, but noticed that Elena was taking an inordinately long time. When she came out, one look at her eyes told him that she had gone in there to weep in private. Again, she kept her pain to herself. The subject of Helen Dawson's tragedy was not mentioned again that evening.

Only three months later, Bea, with her usual "sensitivity," stopped by Elena's room to say, "Carlo and I are going to California tomorrow for a week. Veronica can take care of you while we're away." Then, with a sneer, she added, "By the way, about your friend, Helen Dawson. She's dead!"

With that said, she turned on her heels and marched back to her bedroom.

Jean-Paul and Christopher stopped by later on. They told Elena, "Helen went peacefully during the night, surrounded with love. She will be cremated, and knowing how close to her we were, the family has asked us if we would take possession of the ashes."

Finally, in order to divert Elena's attention from the tragic news of the day, Jean-Paul started reminiscing about the good times the three of them had had traveling around the world. That always brought a smile to Elena's face.

Elena said, "I don't know why, but Hawaii was the best."

Together, the boys said, "We agree!"

They stayed long enough to order some food in for the three of them. It was never easy for them to leave their friend alone with Carlo and Bea, but they knew that there was no way they could alter the situation.

Occasionally Jean-Paul and Christopher would gingerly open the door to the living room or library and try to identify the latest work of art that had mysteriously disappeared. The rooms looked sadly empty, while the clutter on the dining room table made it difficult to discern if there was a priceless bauble surreptitiously hidden next to a frying pan.

The vitrines in Elena's room were no longer lit, but there were only a few objects left to light. And everything was filthy. When Elena was not looking, Jean-Paul would go over to her dresser, which held a silver-framed photograph of Angelina posing in her wedding dress, next to one of a much younger Elena on the day she married Philip, and slide his finger through the dust in disbelief. Even the upholstery on the chair he usually sat in was covered with a towel in order to hide what looked like a slash in the fabric.

—

Whatever the Manzianos were up to, they had one more unexpected hurdle to overcome in their quest for the riches they had coveted for twenty years. It was 1992, and Elena, at seventy-three, was very much alive, but still a virtual prisoner in her own room. Her only visitors were the hairdresser who came twice a week, and, of course, Jean-Paul and Christopher when they were in town. But each time they entered the apartment it became more painful to see the deterioration of the opulence that had once surrounded their friend.

Carlo and Bea's worst nightmare came true the day that Angelina called Elena and said, "Mother, Mark just lost his battle with that awful disease. He finally died of kidney failure. Can Gregorio and I come to New York and stay with you for a while? Mark had written a play that some producers are interested in putting on in New York. We need to have a meeting with them before they lose interest. It would be a wonderful memorial to Mark if we could pull it off."

"I'm so sorry about Mark. Of course, you can come any time you want to."

"We'd like to fly out this weekend and have a business meeting on Monday."

"I'll have the guestrooms ready when you arrive. I can't wait to see you both. 'Bye."

Elena then called Carlo on the intercom and dropped the bomb, "Carlo, I hope you and Bea don't mind, but Angelina just lost her husband and she and Gregorio are coming to visit for a few days. Do you think that Veronica could get the guestrooms ready for them?"

Carlo's nervous giggle took over as he answered, "I don't know, Elena. The rooms need a lot of work and Veronica is alone. There's always the laundress, Ching Mai, who could help, but it's an awful inconvenience. It'll also cost more money to have them work overtime in order to get the rooms ready. I'll see what Bea has to say."

For once, Elena lost it. In spite of the Manzianos best efforts, she still had some fight left in her.

"Angelina and Gregorio are coming this weekend even if I have to make the beds and clean the rooms myself. Do you understand? I don't care how we do it, but it will be done!"

All she heard before slamming down the phone was Carlo's nervous giggle.

Bea, who had overheard the conversation, was fit to be tied, and lost as to what they could do with her debris.

"Carlo, why don't we call the superintendent and ask for another storage room in the basement?"

"But Bea, we need at least two more storage rooms for all of your things. Don't forget, we have to put back some of the precious objects we stashed away in the apartment. Angelina will surely notice the artwork that you hid in the hall closets."

"You had better bring it back out in the open, you stupid man. It's a good thing we didn't send them to California with my other things."

As usual, Carlo took the brunt of the blame whenever anything went wrong.

—

When Angelina and Gregorio arrived, they could tell that Carlo and Bea had had the apartment "surface cleaned" for them. Bea made the supreme effort to be present, although still in her bathrobe, to greet them.

The Manzianos were on their best behavior and even went through the pretense of a normal family dinner.

When the theatrical producer arrived on Monday, Angelina and Gregorio sat with him in the living room, talking about venues and the possible cost of a production in New York.

Bea, who had retreated back to her bedroom after the first day's obligatory appearance, suddenly popped into the living room during the meeting and said, "Excuse me, Angelina, but I wonder if there's enough turkey left over to make some soup."

"I think so, Bea, but I'll check and see after we're through here."

Bea thanked Angelina and left the room only to return a few minutes later to say, "Gregorio, I wonder if you want me to tell Ching Mai to launder the clothes you left out last night."

Gregorio graciously answered, "Thank you Bea, that would be nice."

It seemed as though Bea found a reason to interrupt the meeting every five minutes with a senseless question. Her reason was not just to be a nuisance, but was born from a fear that Elena might be asked to invest money in the play—something that Bea would not be able to tolerate.

After Bea had made at least a half dozen unnecessary trips into the living room to stop the meeting in its tracks, Gregorio knew that he had to put an end to the constant interruptions.

In the most firm yet still polite tone of voice that he could muster in the face of his frustration, he said, "Bea, would you please leave us alone until our meeting is over? We can't get anything done as long as you come in every few minutes and interrupt our train of thought."

Finally Bea had the ammunition she needed. She immediately ran to Carlo and said, "Gregorio has threatened to kill me! He's a dangerous young man. I want you to sit down right now and write a note to Elena telling her how frightened we are. And you can add that even the laundress, Ching Mai is afraid of him!"

As had happened countless times before, it came down to, "If you don't get rid of these people—your daughter and grandson—we'll go away and you'll be all alone in the world." Carlo and Bea knew that once Elena had become too vulnerable to fight back, the best weapon to make her comply with their every wish was to threaten to go away and leave her to fend for herself. Although Elena was suspicious of Bea and knew what a difficult and neurotic woman she was, she still refused to believe that her own brother could be as Machiavellian as his wife.

From that day on it was a house under siege. Bea didn't need much to build a case on and once she started on a mission, she never let up until she had won. She felt that Elena's daughter and grandson stood in the way of everything she wanted. The fact that she and Carlo were now well into their seventies and had no children to benefit from their wealth made no difference; pure greed had blinded them to all common sense and morality.

Gregorio was relieved when the time came to leave his grandmother's house of horrors and take his mother back to her home in California; after that, his work would keep him traveling through Latin America for most of the year. Angelina decided that the only thing she could now do for her mother was to call once a week and let her know that she loved her.

Now the Manzianos believed that they would have full access to all of Elena's assets.

CHAPTER 18

After Angelina and Gregorio left Elena's apartment, the Manzianos were once again free to fill every possible space with anything that Bea could not throw out—which was almost everything that came into the house.

Slowly, Elena became convinced that she really was poor and began to live a life in which Carlo and Bea finally deprived her of every luxury and pleasure that might have brought a semblance of joy into her lonely days.

When Elena noticed that her towels were thread-bare, she asked Carlo, "There's almost nothing left of my towels. Do you think we could get some new ones?"

"If you're sure that it's necessary, I'll ask Bea to buy some for you."

Bea, of course, sent Carlo out to buy his sister's towels. The day they arrived, Bea told Carlo, "I'll take care of them. She doesn't really need them yet. Maybe I'll give them to her in six months when all of the others are in tatters. We mustn't spoil her too much or she'll expect a lot more."

Six months later Bea took them for herself.

The same thing happened when Elena said, "I really need a couple of new nightgowns. The ones I have are full of holes. It's embarrassing for me when Jean-Paul and Christopher come over. I don't want Sheila to see me looking like a baglady, either, when she does my hair. The other day my robe came open and the manicurist was appalled at the condition of my gown."

Again, Carlo said, "Of course we'll see to it that you look presentable. I'll check if they're having a sale at Bloomingdales."

The new nightgowns never arrived.

Bea then called up an old friend of Elena's who sold pot-pourri and scents, and said, "Don't sell anything to Mrs. Zimmerman. She doesn't have any more money. However, you can make up the same scents Mrs. Zimmerman used and send them to me."

The woman was polite but firm, "I'm sorry, Mrs. Manziano, but if I can't make up those scents for Mrs. Zimmerman, then I can't make them up for you. Excuse me, but I have other clients to attend to. Goodbye."

Anyone who had a brain in their head could tell what Carlo and Bea were up to, although no one had yet fathomed the extent of their plundering. Only Jean-Paul and Christopher understood Elena's vulnerability.

Elena's two "boys" were not only increasingly horrified at the condition of the apartment but became truly alarmed when they noticed a Renoir missing from Elena's bedroom. When the time came to make their way back to the front door in the dark ("Electricity costs money"), Jean-Paul whispered to Christopher, "Let's check out the living room and see if the porcelain de Sévres is still there."

Christopher, the more cautious of the two, said, "What if they come out of their rooms and find us?

We can't just rummage around the apartment any way we please."

"Come on, you chicken. I'm only going to look in from the doorway. Oh, Lord, this is what I suspected. There are only a few pieces left. Holy cow, and those bastards are telling Elena that she can't afford new towels or a nightgown. So many priceless objects that she willed to the museum are gone. Even the Louis XVI clock is missing. Where the hell is it all going to?"

"One guess is all you get," answered Christopher. "The old sons of bitches are stashing it away for themselves. If Elena knew the half of it, she would be devastated. But we both know that they would soon convince her that they're devoting themselves to saving her from dire poverty. It's all probably hidden around here somewhere in the midst of the junk, and if necessary they can pull it out at a moment's notice."

"Come on, let's get out of here. This is depressing. There's not much we can do right now but stay out of trouble with Carlo and Bea and not abandon Elena. Karma has a great way of working out in the end. Hell, these assholes are over eighty years old now. The big mystery is what do they think they're going to get out of living this way for so many years while waiting for someone to die?"

~

In 1999, there was no one but Jean-Paul and Christopher for Elena to celebrate her eightieth birthday with. She wasn't too thrilled about the number eighty, but, as always, she laughed and smiled when they brought out champagne and a tin of the caviar she and Christopher had always loved. Champagne and caviar were not Jean-Paul's favorite things in the world, but he was delighted to see Elena enjoying being pampered once again. The boys knew how to spoil her with little luxuries she had gone without for so long.

After the first glass, Elena suddenly turned serious and said, "Jean-Paul, I hate having to do this, but I wonder if you could do me a favor."

"Of course, Elena. Anything in the world you want is yours. You know how good you've always been to everyone."

"I don't know how to say this, but could you lend me fifteen hundred dollars? I promise that I'll find a way to pay you back."

For the rest of her life Elena never got over the fact that Jean-Paul got up, went over to her desk and wrote her a check for the full amount—all without saying a word.

And it was that way every time she asked.

He could only imagine Elena's humiliation at having to beg for money. Jean-Paul knew that this would be the only way that Elena could have her hairdresser and manicurist come to the house when she needed them. The only thing that infuriated him was that Carlo and Bea were the ones who had created this senseless scenario. There was plenty of money somewhere, but the Manzianos were hoarding it for themselves.

～

It was in Elena's eightieth year that, while walking around her bed, she tripped on a corner of the comforter, which had slipped down to the floor. Her right shoulder took the brunt of the fall. It was the faithful Veronica who heard her cries, found her lying on the floor, and went to rouse Carlo and Bea from their rooms.

"Dr. Manziano, Mrs. Manziano, please come quickly. Mrs. Zimmerman has fallen and hurt herself. I can't get her up and she's in terrible pain."

"Carlo, don't you dare go to her. She's only looking for sympathy. Let Veronica take care of her," hissed a secretly pleased Bea.

After getting no response from behind the locked door to the Manzianos' suite, Veronica ran back to Elena's room and cried, "They don't answer their door when I knock, Mrs. Zimmerman. What do you want me to do now? Do you think anything's broken? Shall I call Mr. Jean-Paul or Sheila? She's supposed to come and do your hair today."

At that moment, as if on cue, Sheila walked into Elena's bedroom; the Manzianos had ordered the front door to be unlocked at all times so that they would never have to be disturbed. The only doors that were locked were the ones leading to their own quarters, and to the many closets that they had appropriated for themselves throughout the apartment.

"Mrs. Zimmerman," cried Sheila, "what happened to you? Do you think you can at least get on the bed?"

"I'm sorry, Sheila," moaned Elena, "but I think I broke my shoulder. I don't think I can get up at all. Please call my brother. He's a doctor and should know what to do."

"I don't know why, but they're not answering their door. We have no way of reaching them unless we break it down. Let me try the intercom.... No, they're not answering that either. I think we have to call 911 for an ambulance. We have to take you to the Emergency Room at New York Hospital right away."

While Sheila was dialing 911, Elena looked up at Veronica's anguished face and whispered, "Please call Jean-Paul and Christopher and ask them to meet us at the Emergency Room."

"Right away, Mrs. Zimmerman."

When the ambulance arrived, it was difficult to put Elena on the gurney without causing too much agony. But she had a high threshold for pain, and the paramedics knew their job. Within a few minutes they arrived at the hospital. Although Philip had been dead for many years, the Zimmerman name was still impressive, and Elena was put in a VIP part of the Emergency Room.

Jean-Paul arrived at the Emergency Room a short while later and told the woman at the desk that he was Mrs. Zimmerman's son.

He spoke with the doctor in the hallway outside her door. The doctor said, "I'm afraid that your mother has broken her shoulder. We'll be taking her for an X-ray in a few minutes. By the way, has she been drinking today? Her speech is extremely slurred and hard to understand."

Jean-Paul explained, "No, Doctor, she has not been drinking. The reason that she tripped so easily and speaks the way she does, is because of brain damage that occurred when she fell down a flight of stairs in 1969."

"I understand. Does she have any other serious health problems I should know about at this time?"

"I can't think of any, Doctor. She may be incapacitated to a certain degree, but otherwise she's in good health for an eighty-year-old woman."

The doctor looked stunned for a moment and then consulted his papers before exclaiming, "My God, I can't believe it. To look at her, one would think that she was half that age. She's so beautiful. But don't worry, we'll take good care of her. By the way, does she have a Living Will?"

"Yes, she does. I have it right here."

When Harry Haimoff had prepared Elena's will, she had made out a Living Will and had named Jean-Paul as her medical proxy, because, as Elena said, "You'll know what I would want."

After Elena had gone for X-rays, the doctor told Jean-Paul, "I'm afraid that the break is quite severe. We're going to have to operate. The surgeon has arrived and we are preparing Mrs. Ziimmerman right now. You can go in and see her for a few minutes. We gave her something for the pain. I don't know how much use she will have of that arm and hand, but we're going to do our best. You can also speak to the surgeon, if you wish."

"I think I'll wait till after the operation to speak to the surgeon. Right now I'd like to see my mother, if I may. Thank you, Doctor."

"Come with me, then. I'll take you to her."

Elena lay on the gurney, looking pale but unbelievably beautiful. Jean-Paul took her hand and said, "Elena, I'm going to remain right here until the operation is over. And once you recuperate we'll celebrate with more champagne and caviar than you could ever imagine."

"I don't know what I would do without you. Would you please call Angelina and tell her how clumsy her mother was today? But please don't upset her. Just tell her I'm going to be fine."

She blew him a kiss as they rolled her into the operating room.

～

Christopher joined his partner in the waiting room and was there when Carlo burst in with his nervous giggle and asked in his brusque way, "Well, what's going on?"

He asked no questions about the accident or how Elena was feeling. And he gave no explanation as to what he and his wife had been up to while Elena was lying on the floor in agony, waiting for help to arrive. It was as though this whole episode had been a great inconvenience to the Manzianos and the only thing that they cared about was, "Is she dead yet?"

Jean-Paul explained politely, "Elena tripped and fell in her room and fractured a part of her shoulder and upper arm. She's now in the operating room, where the surgeon is trying to fix the damage."

The two young men kept a calm demeanor while talking to the old man, since they knew that throttling him would not benefit them or Elena. Whenever they ran into Carlo or Bea, they always remained charming so that the Manzianos would not suspect that they were onto them.

While Carlo sat with them in the waiting room, Jean-Paul and Christopher got their first inkling that Carlo's mind was not so clear any more. In spite of his bluster, the eighty-four-year-old man seemed confused and not really sure of why he was there.

After four hours, the surgeon came in and said, "I'm happy to say that Mrs. Zimmerman is doing well. She's in the recovery room now and the nurse will take you in to see her in a little while. We did the best we could, but as we told you earlier, she may not recover the full use of her right arm or hand. She'll need some help caring for herself, especially since she is right-handed. Do you have any questions?"

Carlo said nothing, so Jean-Paul asked, "How long do you think Mrs. Zimmerman will be in the hospital, Doctor?"

"At least a couple of weeks, and then she'll need some physical therapy."

Finally Carlo spoke up. "That should all cost a bit of money."

"I assume that Mrs. Zimmerman has insurance that will cover most of the medical expenses. But at her age, she will need someone to care for her at home. Of course, that all depends on how well the arm heals."

"Thank you, Doctor," said Jean-Paul and Christopher in unison. As usual, Carlo was at a loss for words and said nothing. The boys figured that he was worried about telling Bea that Elena might be incurring some expenses in the future.

~

A little while later, the boys leaned over Elena's bed as she opened her eyes.

"How do you feel?"

Elena gave them a little smile and her usual answer, "Great!" Then she added, "I feel as though we've already started on the champagne."

Later, Sheila walked in and told the boys, "Why don't you both go home? I'll take over for a while. You had a long wait during the operation, but I'm here now and I'll keep you posted. By the way, where is Dr. Manziano? He should be here to see his sister."

Christopher spoke up and said, "He left as soon as the doctor told us that the operation was a success. I think Bea must be anxiously waiting for him at home."

That line brought a huge eye roll from the patient.

On their way out of the hospital they ran into Carlo, who seemed lost and confused as he roamed the hallways trying to find a way out. The boys weren't even sure that he knew where he was or how to get home.

"Carlo, come with us. We'll drop you off at the apartment."

He looked at them as though his world was slightly out of focus, and followed them like a child out of the hospital and into a taxi. By this time they were sure that Carlo was no longer completely competent. He was still alert enough to be a threat, especially with Bea ordering him around, but something was obviously very wrong with Elena's brother.

—

Bea's reaction when her husband came home was, "This is perfect. If Elena's right arm and hand are not functioning properly, she has to give you her power of attorney. Then you can sign all her checks and any documents we want. No problem!"

Elena had several visitors while she lay in her hospital bed. She had been kind to many people during her lifetime and had always been more than generous to those around her. But Jean-Paul and Christopher were a bit uneasy when they saw that the two of them were the only ones who had not worked for Elena or benefited monetarily from being around her. All her other "friends" had long since fallen away, when Mrs. Zimmerman was no longer of use to them. Only the potential parasites remained.

When Elena came home from the hospital, she had already been practicing writing her name. She must have written it over a hundred times. Elena Zimmerman… Elena Zimmerman… Elena Zimmerman…

But however well Elena could write her name, she was still unsteady on her feet. Taking a bath was a nearly impossible and dangerous feat.

"Carlo, please. If nothing else, I desperately need an aide around the clock. I'm even frightened to walk to the toilet by myself, especially at night. And unless you and Bea are willing to take on a twenty-four-hour-a-day job of caring for me, I need some help."

Since neither of the Manzianos was interested in caring for a semi-invalid, Elena got her wish. Bea had a tantrum, but saw no other way out. The next day, two aides were hired to be with Elena. Each had a twelve-hour shift, five days a week. Two other aides came to fill in on the weekends. They made it clear after the first five minutes that they were there to see to Mrs. Zimmerman's needs and not Mrs. Manziano's. It was certainly not a taxing job, since Elena had never been a demanding woman.

When the cable to Elena's television, her only form of entertainment, broke down, the daytime aide, Marlene, found Bea in the kitchen and said, "Excuse me, Mrs. Manziano, but Mrs. Zimmerman's television cable is not working. Do you think Dr. Manziano could call someone up and have it repaired?"

"Don't you ever bother my husband with anything like that again. You can ask the superintendent. But my sister-in-law's cable television is not our affair." Having said her piece, she stormed off to her bedroom.

Bea knew that it would now be discovered that she and Carlo had never given any Christmas bonuses to the Superintendent or elevator men—something that is routinely expected in that kind of building. But what the Manzianos didn't know was that Elena secretly gave bonuses to the building staff every year from whatever money she could get from the sale of a piece of jewelry or a "loan" from Jean-Paul.

Marlene, who was a compassionate woman, threw herself on the mercy of the building superintendent, and he soon had someone in to fix Elena's cable. Elena had been lucky in the choice of aides who came to care for her. Not only were they exceptionally caring, but intelligent as well. Within a short period of time, they fell under Elena's spell and became exceedingly protective of their patient.

On warm spring days, Jean-Paul and Christopher would come to visit. "Come on Elena, we'll make you beautiful, seat you in your wheelchair like a queen, and go for a spin in Central Park. After all, it's just across the street. We're sure that Marlene would also like some fresh air today."

The introduction of a wheelchair into Elena's life had been both a blessing and a reminder of her increasing infirmity—something she accepted with grace. For Carlo and Bea, however, it was another way to cut corners. Whenever Elena had a doctor's appointment, they would refuse to hire a car to take her. Instead, no matter how far away it was, they would tell Marlene, "You can wheel her in her chair!"

~

Everyone in the apartment was getting older, including Carlo and Bea, who had not counted on Elena's incredible recuperative power. Bea had to wait another two years for Carlo to be given power of attorney over his sister's affairs.

By then, Carlo was even less lucid, and Bea actually had moments when she seemed to believe that she had become the young, rich, and gorgeous Elena Zimmerman. When she came back to reality, she was filled with a rage that made her increasingly dangerous to Elena.

The faithful aides, who had no love for the Manzianos, became even more vigilant in their protection of Elena.

But Elena was still, even in her progressively more fragile state, nobody's fool.

CHAPTER 19

The year 2001 was not a good one for Elena. On a chilly February morning, Jean-Paul received a frantic call from Marlene. "Please, Mr. Jean-Paul, Mrs. Zimmerman is asking for you. She's in an awful state. I've never seen her so upset. Her daughter just called to say that she has ovarian cancer. She's going to be operated on this week. The only person Mrs. Zimmerman wants to see is you. Can you come now?"

"Of course, Marlene. I'll be there right away."

After having spent years doing concerts, cabaret, and recordings, Jean-Paul was not an early riser and usually needed a little time to pull himself together. However, he quickly popped into the shower, shaved, dressed, and ran over to Elena's house. He knew that Elena never inflicted her emotional pain on anybody unless it was an emergency.

When he walked down the hall of the once grand Zimmerman apartment to Elena's bedroom, he could see the back of the tiny figure hunched over in the wheelchair. She sat inches from the television, which had been turned off. Her once perfectly-coiffed blonde hair was now dyed a mousy brown, and simple bangs on her forehead replaced the glamorous curls that had framed her face.

"Elena, I came as soon as I could. How are you? And what's the matter with Angelina?"

By this time Elena's enormous willpower and need for denial had started to kick in. She looked tired, but was no longer the hysterical mother crying for her only child. Everything else had been taken away from her by Carlo and Bea, and now she would not accept the fact that she might lose the one thing that she held dearest in the world. Jean-Paul had once believed that Elena had superhuman powers to overcome any obstacle and, in her own way, she had believed it, too.

"I don't know, Jean-Paul. Angelina is being operated on this week. Maybe it's not as bad as we think. You know how she always looks on the gloomy side of things. There has to be hope. Maybe we'll find out that it's all a big mistake."

Whatever the story was, Elena was once again in control of herself, and Jean-Paul realized that he had missed that small window of opportunity when she had let her guard down.

All he could do now was encourage her to be optimistic—the only way that she could survive the day. Tomorrow would bring either relief or more heartbreak, but whichever it was, Jean-Paul knew that he had to get his friend through the immediate crisis.

"Elena, let's not be hasty in expecting the worst. If it really is cancer, there have been many new scientific advances in recent years. What were once hopeless cases are now being completely cured. I think it's too soon for any of us to jump to conclusions. For whatever it's worth, you know you can call us at any time of the day or night. We'll be here!"

He stayed as long as he felt that he could do some good, and then went home to call Angelina in California.

"Angie, it's Jean-Paul. I just came from your mother's house. What's this I hear about your being ill?"

"It's true, Jean-Paul. I had trouble with my bowels for a while and thought it was just constipation. When other symptoms started to develop, I went to the doctor, who diagnosed ovarian cancer. I'm afraid that it's stage four. I doubt that even with an operation I have a great deal of time left. They also warned me that, depending on how far the cancer has spread, I may have to have a colostomy bag. Gregorio is flying in tonight to be with me. He said that when I'm better, he'll take me to see the beautiful places in Europe that I visited with Mummy and Daddy when I was young. I look forward to that. But, you know, I've been so lonely since Mark died that I sometimes sit alone at the kitchen table and scream, just to hear a human voice."

Angelina then asked her oldest friend, "Jean-Paul, when the time comes, will you be there to help me die?"

Jean-Paul fought back the tears when he answered, "Of course, Angie, I'll be there."

And that's how the conversation ended.

Within a week, Angelina had been given the worst possible diagnosis. It definitely was stage four cancer, and when she woke up from the operation, she was faced with having to deal with a colostomy bag. She actually took the bad news with a great deal of courage and immediately made plans for the trip to Europe with Gregorio. Nothing was going to stop her from living right up to the end. And she was determined to do it her way.

When it came to chemotherapy and radiation, she said, "My quality of life is more important than the quantity. I will accept a light form of chemotherapy. I have no desire to spend more time being sick from the treatment than from the disease. Lord knows that I've never been inordinately vain, but I don't want to lose my hair."

Her oncologist was understanding, and said, "As long as you make an informed decision, you have the right to choose the path that you're most comfortable with."

As far as Jean-Paul and Christopher knew, Angelina did not complain or make her mother suffer unduly with the gruesome reality of the illness. Angelina called every Sunday and spoke to Elena for about a half an hour, with Angie doing most of the talking. They talked about the languages that Angelina was studying and the choral group that she had joined. In essence, Angelina went on with her life. Though it was still lonely when she came home at the end of the day, she knew that Gregorio would be by her side whenever she needed support.

But there was no such support for Elena at the end of the day. Carlo and Bea still stayed in their rooms while Marlene ordered dinner for Elena from the local coffee shop.

~

Christopher and Jean-Paul came to visit Elena whenever they could, something that always brought a smile to their friend's face. Although she never complained, it was evident that Angelina's illness had deeply disturbed Elena. It had affected her physically as well as emotionally.

When Jean-Paul walked into her room one afternoon, Marlene was helping Elena out of the bathroom and across the bedroom to her wheelchair. He saw in one quick glance that Marlene was mostly carrying her, since her right leg did not seem to be functioning.

In order to cover an awkward moment that Elena would have hated, Jean-Paul quickly retreated into the hallway and waited until Elena was seated. Then he burst into the room as though he had seen nothing of the new infirmity that he knew his friend would not want to dwell on with anyone, not even her closest friend.

To the question, "How are you," Elena gave him her dazzling smile and the usual, "Great!"

While they talked, Jean-Paul noticed to his dismay that Elena's right hand lay limply in her lap. He suspected that she had had a stroke, since she never moved her hand the whole time he was there. He knew then that Carlo must have finally acquired his sister's power of attorney and was free to write checks any way he and Bea wished.

—

"Carlo, we have to be careful now not to arouse any suspicion. Do you think that that meddlesome Jean-Paul has any idea of what has gone on in this house? He's not blind, you know. Anyway, now her accounts can be manipulated more easily than before. And we can always say that the artwork had to be sold to pay the bills. We're finally nearing the finish line!"

"But Bea, we should still be careful and keep the things we hid under lock and key. I only hope that we can soon sell the porcelain de Sévres. The only problem is that it's so prominently displayed in the apartment that its absence is sure to be noticed."

"You stupid man, nothing can touch us. We've made it this far and we'll make it all the way—all the way to the bank!"

"Bea, sometimes you make me so mad when you call me stupid. I'm not stupid. And if you want more prescriptions, you had better treat me with a little more respect. The way you treat me, I'm not sure that I love you anymore. As a matter of fact, I don't love you. Period."

"Oh, Carlo, sometimes you're like a temperamental teenager. I don't know why I put up with you. Now let's see how we can transfer the last check from the Zimmerman Trust into my account. You put it in yours the last time. What is it, two hundred thousand dollars this time?"

It was amazing that these two aged crooks didn't stop to think that they had now spent thirty years plotting the big payoff. And they never even considered that there might be consequences to their actions—money and artwork didn't just disappear with no questions asked. There would inevitably come a time when they would have to answer to a government agency, a bank or a relative. But by this time, Carlo and Bea had left the world of reality and retreated into a world in which they had both become untouchable.

The two rarely made an appearance in Elena's room. The well groomed woman that Bea had once been was now a harridan who wore no makeup to hide the ravages of drugs and alcohol, and her long dirty white hair hung down to her shoulders. She spent her days dressed in the disintegrating red silk bathrobe that she had pulled from Elena's wastebasket years ago.

One day when Jean-Paul was sitting with Elena in her room, he caught a glimpse of Bea peeking into Elena's room from the hallway outside. On one of Bea's rare forays out of her room, she had heard voices coming from her sister-in-law's room and had come to see who the interloper might be.

Jean-Paul refused to let her think that she was clever enough to sneak away without being seen.

"Hi, Bea," he called out, with a big smile on his face.

"Hello, Jean-Paul," Bea replied girlishly. She now had no choice but to acknowledge her presence. "I heard voices and thought it might be you. How have you been?" she asked as she sashayed through the doorway like a coy five-year-old. She did everything but twist her stringy hair around her fingers as a child would.

She reminded Jean-Paul of Bette Davis as the crazed old woman reliving her childhood stardom in the movie, Whatever Happened to Baby Jane?

"You look very handsome in that Gianni Versace jacket. I'll bet you and Christopher keep that company in business," cooed Bea.

"Well, one of the things that Elena taught me was how to buy the best. You look wonderful too, Bea. It's nice to have seen you. Give my best to Carlo," answered Jean-Paul with relief as she turned to go.

Naturally the whole scene called for a big eye roll from Elena.

—

It was around this time that both of Elena's boys noticed a marked decrease in her ability to speak. Before, they had been able to decipher whatever she said, with a modicum of difficulty. Now there were times when it became nearly impossible to understand her. But instead of making a tragic spectacle out of Elena's problem, Jean-Paul would laugh and say, "Huh?"

Elena fell right into the spirit of things and tried again. If she was not understood the second time around, they would laugh again when he gave an even louder, "HUH??"

He knew that there was nothing she hated more than people who tried to humor her by pretending to understand what she was saying. She far preferred the truth, especially when it came from someone she loved.

The only thing left for them to do was play their own form of charades until she got her point across. Elena was not one for self-pity or any kind of pretension.

⁓

"Carlo!"

"Yes, Bea."

"Did you put our monthly check for twenty-five thousand dollars in the bank yet?"

"Yes, Bea. You never stop hounding me. And don't worry, the other two hundred thousand dollars went into my account this time."

"What's this I hear about Elena asking for more than the five hundred we give her every month for her hair, makeup and nails? She should be happy to get it. After all, she doesn't go anywhere."

"What?" asked an increasingly deaf Carlo.

"You stupid man, now you can't hear me anymore. What good are you, anyway? You know you peed on the couch the other night while you were sleeping. Now I'm stuck with both a crippled old woman and a deaf old fool. I promise you, life isn't going to be this way much longer."

Not having heard any of Bea's latest diatribe, Carlo meekly said, "I'll go in and talk to Elena about curbing her expenses with the hairdresser."

It took Carlo a while to unlock and relock the doors to their quarters before going down the hall to Elena's bedroom. God forbid someone should walk in and see the overwhelming clutter that he and Bea were living in.

"Elena, I wanted to talk to you about the money you spend on yourself every month. You know that you can't go on this way. You have to face the fact that there's no money left."

Elena pleaded one more time, "I know I have no more money, but could we buy a small jar of face cream for Sheila's birthday? It's just a small gift that I know she would enjoy."

Carlo could do nothing but shake his head and say, "You know we can't afford it, Elena. The aides are eating up all that's left of your money."

"Well, can you tell me if there's any champagne left in the liquor closet? The only thing that I enjoy is having a glass in the evening before my dinner."

"What's that about a sinner?"

"Carlo, I said dinner not sinner. Why don't you get yourself a hearing aid?" screamed Elena.

"I don't need a hearing aid. I can hear anything I want to."

After another nervous giggle, he left a confused Elena alone in her room.

—

Although Elena still thought of Jean-Paul and Christopher as "her boys," her best friends were now sixty years old. Although their hair had turned salt-and-pepper grey, they had retained their youthful looks. Cosmetic surgery had not been necessary. They both had good genes.

Jean-Paul had stopped singing professionally a few years before. He had long since passed the young heartthrob stage, and felt that he had accomplished most of his goals. Whenever he sang now, it was for charity. One reason that he was able to leave the world of show business was that both his parents had died in a private plane crash and had left him independently wealthy. Now he found a new way to express himself musically by singing in soup kitchens and hospices for the sick and dying. The emotional impact of the charitable use of his talent was more powerful than any applause he had received in theaters around the world.

As far as his parents were concerned, he felt that, although they had gone too soon, they would have wished to die together. Such was the strength of the bond that had tied them together for a lifetime.

Elena's daughter, Angelina, was doing well on her light chemotherapy and continued her interest in languages and music. She had enough energy to do the things that were important to her. And the trip to Europe with Gregorio had been a great success. She had gone to all the museums that she had enjoyed visiting with her parents as a young girl. Angelina was making the most of the time she had left.

Elena, who had been so generous with her friends and family over a lifetime, was still at the mercy of Carlo and Bea. If it had not been for Jean-Paul and Christopher, her life would have been unbearable. As it was, she endured humiliation after humiliation with the greatest grace, never complaining and always making the most of whatever time she had with "her boys." They still laughed together and talked about old times—good times you only share with people you love. Sometimes Gregorio passed through town, and spent as much time as he could with the remarkable woman he was proud to call his grandmother.

⁓

In October of 2004, Jean-Paul and Christopher arrived in Elena's room with a bottle of champagne and said, "Elena, do you know what we're going to celebrate today?"

"No, Jean-Paul, but I'd be happy to celebrate anything with the two of you."

"It was fifty years ago that we met. However, it's been only thirty-five years that you've known Christopher. Do you think that that's a long enough time for him to celebrate with us?"

"He'd better!" answered Elena. "But I can't believe how the time has flown. I remember the first time you walked into the apartment as though it were yesterday. My God, you were adorable. Let's drink to that!"

⁓

Carlo and Bea were still hiding out in their rooms, amassing as much of Elena's artwork and cash as they could, while they continued to tell her that she was broke.

Jean-Paul was the one who came to Elena's rescue every time she needed cash. Finally, in order not to embarrass her any more than necessary, he would discreetly place cash in the pocket of her robe when he kissed her goodbye. Sometimes he and Christopher would see something that she needed and buy it as a gift. Once, he saw a long pearl necklace in a store window and bought it for her as an "un-birthday gift."

In April of 2005, Jean-Paul received a note from Elena, written by her aide, since she had not regained the use of her right hand. It said,

> *Dear Jean-Paul,*
> *I know I've borrowed money from you in the last few years and never paid you back. I don't know how I could pay back any of it unless I sell my body. I've sold almost everything I own. Now I'm defunct.*

I've found $100. Let me know how much I owe you.

Love, Love

Elena

Later that day, he said to Elena, "Please forget about any money that's passed between us. A son doesn't ask his mother to pay him back."

On one of Jean-Paul and Christopher's frequent visits to Elena in her lonely sanctuary, when they leaned over her wheelchair to kiss her goodbye, she said, "There's nobody left, but I know I have the two of you. I love you."

~

The elderly man and woman with no conscience who lived in the same apartment with Elena might have stolen her worldly possessions, but they hadn't taken away her heart—something that had always been the most valuable part of Elena. And if Carlo and Bea thought that they had reached the final chapter of the story, they were sorely mistaken and in for the surprise of their lives.

CHAPTER 20

When Elena's aide, Marlene, saw Bea and Carlo carrying the precious porcelain de Sévres piece by piece into the dining room and putting it on the massive table, she knew that Carlo and Bea were up to no good. She also wondered what they had done with the mounds of miscellaneous things that had covered the top of the table, until she saw a dozen or so large packing boxes that had been sealed and pushed to the side of the room.

"Mrs. Zimmerman, I hate to bother you," said Marlene, "but do you know that Dr. and Mrs. Manziano have taken all of the porcelain that you had in the living room and laid it out on the dining room table? I know how much it means to you, and I wonder if they are planning to sell it."

"Thank you Marlene," said Elena in as calm a voice as possible. "Do you think that you could wheel my chair into the dining room, please?"

"Of course, Mrs. Zimmerman. But please don't let them know that I was the one who told you. You know how difficult Mrs. Manziano can be under the best of circumstances."

"Don't worry, Marlene. This time they're going to have to answer to me. No one else need be involved. How dare they think that they can take my property and do what they like, without even consulting me." She had been too cowed by her brother to let the old Elena emerge—the one who feared nothing and no one.

But this time Carlo and Bea had gone too far. Elena almost enjoyed the feeling of going into battle with these people who had made her life so miserable. She had nothing to lose anymore. Finally, she understood how little they cared about her welfare. It was all about them.

The looks on both their faces, along with her brother's nervous giggle, said it all. In her quest to satisfy her family, something that had been instilled in her from birth, she had handed over her own life to people who had only used her beauty, money, and power for their own purposes.

"I was going to talk to you later on," stammered Carlo.

"I think we can talk right now," answered Elena with a look that froze Carlo and Bea to the spot.

Bea made a pathetic attempt at a smile before retreating behind Carlo, who was more useless than ever.

"We thought it might be best if we sold the porcelain to pay the bills. You know how little money is left."

"I don't want to hear how little money is left. I want to know how you can be so cavalier about my belongings without even consulting me. And by the way, the porcelain is going back into the living room where it belongs. Do you understand!" She turned her head toward her aide. "Marlene, please take me back to my room."

Carlo and Bea were powerless to move for several seconds after Elena had been wheeled down the hallway. Then Bea let lose with a torrent of expletives that Elena could hear from her room.

"Carlo, you stupid, stupid man. How could you let this happen? From now on you have to be more careful. There is nothing, I repeat, nothing that is going to keep us from getting the money from the sale of this porcelain. But for the moment you can put it all back in the living room in case she comes out of her room again today."

Once inside her room, Elena asked Marlene to get Harry Haimoff on the phone for her, and to ask him to meet her at a certain spot in Central Park that afternoon. She thought it was time for her brother and sister-in-law to find out that she no longer feared their threats of abandonment. The life that she had been forced to live was far worse than anything that they could try to intimidate her with.

It was not easy for Elena to put herself together in a way that would make her feel comfortable being seen out of the house. But between Sheila and Marlene, she ended up looking like the old Elena. One of her smart Emanuel Ungaro suits still fit, and the spirit in her eyes shone in a way that had been missing for a long time. The doormen and elevator men greeted her warmly. She had always treated them with respect, and they were delighted to see one of their favorite tenants finally emerging from the isolation of her apartment.

Marlene and Sheila sat a couple of benches away from Elena and her lawyer in order to give them privacy. It was a beautiful sunny day—one that gave hope of better days to come.

Meanwhile Carlo and Bea were locked in their rooms, completely unaware that Elena had left the apartment.

About half an hour after Elena had returned from her trek into Central Park and her meeting with the lawyer, the Manzianos received a phone call on their private line from Harry Haimoff himself.

Carlo answered with his usual, "Hell-o," emphasizing the "Hell" before lowering his voice for the "o."

"May I speak to Dr. Manziano, please?" said a polite voice on the other end of the line.

"Yes, this is Dr. Manziano. Who's this?"

"My name is Harry Haimoff and I'm a lawyer who is representing Mrs. Zimmerman. I understand that you have possible plans to sell some of Mrs. Zimmerman's precious items such as her porcelain de Sévres. I must warn you that you are unable to legally sell any of Mrs. Zimmerman's property without her consent. Do you understand?"

"Certainly, we wouldn't dream of doing anything against my sister's wishes."

"Good," said Harry, "then we understand each other, right?"

"Of course. Thank you. By the way, how long have you known my sister?"

"I'm afraid that is privileged information between my client and me. Good day, Doctor."

Carlo hung up the phone with a stunned look on his face.

"What was that all about? And what is this person's connection to Elena?... Carlo, for God's sake answer me, you stupid man."

"That was Elena's lawyer," said Carlo in a voice shaking with fear. He was as frightened of breaking the news to his wife as he was at finding out that Elena was turning the tables on them.

"You mean that cunt has counsel? I don't believe it. We've waited long enough, Carlo. It's finally time to take real action—and you know what I mean!"

"But Bea, I don't know what we should do. Everything has changed. We could get into real trouble."

"You stupid, stupid man. Why did I ever marry you? You're so afraid of your precious little sister. Well, I haven't hung around here all these years for nothing. I'm taking action, whether you like it or not. And there's no time to waste."

Carlo sank down on the urine-soaked couch that Bea insisted he sleep on every night, since the bed was covered with articles that she was hoarding. Every night she moved the four-foot high pile of junk just enough to give her room to lie down on a corner of the mattress.

⌣

"Oh, Marlene, would you be so kind as to give Mrs. Zimmerman these little pills? Dr. Manziano says that they would be good for her."

If Marlene was not suspicious of the pills, the un-characteristic sweetness that went with the request was enough to make the aide promptly flush them down the toilet. She never told Elena about the incident, but warned the other aides and Jean-Paul to discard any medication Bea asked them to give to Elena.

⌣

A few weeks later, Jean-Paul was visiting Elena and ran into Carlo in the hallway leading to her room. He said casually, "Hi, Carlo, this is for you. I thought it would be a good idea for you to have a copy of Elena's Living Will. It gives me the power to make medical decisions on her behalf in case she becomes incapacitated."

Carlo gave Jean-Paul his usual blank look and then ran into the kitchen, where Marlene was having a peaceful cup of tea. Not knowing the hysteria that this piece of paper had just caused in Carlo's confused brain, Jean-Paul continued calmly down the hall for his visit with Elena.

"What is this?" Carlo screamed at Marlene. "Jean-Paul just gave me a will that Elena made out to him! Look at it! It's crazy! Bea is going to kill me! It's not right!"

Knowing that Carlo was in the early stages of senility, Marlene stood up and said, "Please, Dr. Manziano, calm yourself. Let me see what the paper says."

"Here, look at it yourself. He said it was a will of some sort."

One quick glance was all it took for Marlene to understand.

"No, no, Dr. Manziano. You don't understand. It's what is called a Living Will. It only gives the person the right to make medical decisions in case the patient is unable to do so. Don't worry, it takes nothing away from you or your wife."

Carlo understood nothing of what Marlene said to him. All his sense of reasoning had disappeared as soon as he had heard the word "will."

Elena and Jean-Paul were having a quiet talk when Carlo burst into the bedroom with a nervous giggle and an evil smile, and said whatever his muddled brain thought would wound Elena the most. "You know, Elena, that Angelina's cancer is probably going to kill her very soon. It's been four years now and she's already survived longer than anyone expected."

It broke Jean-Paul's heart to see Elena's face contort with pain before she could turn her head away from her brother. "No cancer, no cancer," she said.

"Well, we have to face the facts. She's in stage four and she's probably going to die soon!"

Elena kept her head turned away from this monstrous exhibition of cruelty and just kept repeating, "No cancer, no cancer."

By now Jean-Paul wanted to strangle the giggling man, who was taunting Elena in the cruelest way possible. He couldn't believe that her own brother could be that gratuitously mean to someone who had shown only kindness and compassion to others all her life.

When Jean-Paul saw that Carlo was not going to relent, he knew that the time had come for him to step in and stop the tirade.

In as calm a voice as he could summon up under the circumstances, Jean-Paul said the truth: "I spoke to Angelina last night, and she sounded great!"

Carlo somehow understood that he was outnumbered, and could find nothing else to say except, "Well, have it your way." He walked out with the evil, crazed smile still on his face.

As soon as he was gone, Elena and Jean-Paul resumed their conversation as though nothing had happened.

It was when Jean-Paul was on his way out that Marlene stopped him and explained, "Mr. Jean-Paul, right after you arrived, Dr. Manziano ran into the kitchen in a panic over the Living Will that you gave him. He thought Mrs. Zimmerman was leaving you all her worldly goods. I tried to explain it to him, but he just couldn't understand. Maybe his wife will be able to clarify what a Living Will is really about. I'm sorry he tried to upset Mrs. Zimmerman, but there was no way I could stop him.

Thank God you were there to keep him from torment-
ing her more than he did."

"That's all right, Marlene. We all try to do what we
can for Mrs. Zimmerman. All I ask of you is to keep flush-
ing Mrs. Manziano's little white pills down the toilet. Be
sure that she never gives any to Mrs. Zimmerman."

But he worried that it would be impossible for the
aides to protect Elena twenty-four hours a day. There
would always be the odd moment when the wily Manzianos could have access to their prey.

⁓

A few days later, Carlo and Bea went into the kitchen
where Marlene and the night aide, Margot, were chat-
ting before changing shifts. Bea tried to be charming.

"Oh, Margot, we're so glad that you and Marlene are
both here," said Bea. "I wonder if you would mind signing this little paper for which we need two witnesses.
It's some legal mumbo-jumbo that our lawyer needs by
tomorrow. These details are a nuisance, I know, but we
are doing our best to protect Mrs. Zimmerman in every
way that we can. Would you be so kind as to help us out?
We'd appreciate it so much. Even I'm not too sure what

it's all about myself. Dr. Manziano is the clever one who handles the business end of things, but all you have to do is sign your names right there. You're such angels to do this. We're so lucky to have you both here. Just sign where it says witness."

"But Mrs. Manziano, we can't see the document. It's covered by a sheet of paper. All you're showing us is the place that says witness."

"Oh fiddle-faddle, Margot. It's just a boring piece of paper with some legal talk on it. It's quite all right. Mrs. Zimmerman's lawyer wouldn't ask you to sign anything that would be detrimental to her. Come on, ladies, just sign your full names right here. We don't have all night to discuss it."

Bea was obviously beginning to get irritated at the aides' reluctance to sign her name. Marlene was as unhappy as Margot, but decided that Bea wouldn't hesitate to fire both women in a heartbeat if they didn't sign. In the end, Bea got her way, and bullied both women into signing a document that they were never given the opportunity to read.

Later on, when the couple had returned to their rooms, Bea turned to Carlo and said, "You see, my dear, it's so simple. Now all we have to do is sign Elena's name to this paper and the Zimmerman Trust will be ours when she dies. Carlo! Are you listening to anything I'm saying? You just sit around looking out into space all the time while I do all the work. Oh well, never mind, I'll take care of it myself. After all, my handwriting is almost the same as hers to begin with. Lord, we're almost like twins."

And with that piece of paper, Elena's fate hung in the balance.

CHAPTER 21

On May 11, 2006, five days after Marlene and Margot witnessed the document that Bea had signed Elena's name to, Elena made the mistake of telling Carlo that she had a tummy ache. Minutes after Carlo left the room, Bea rushed in with a glass of water and some little white pills in her hand. Her timing was perfect. At that moment, Margot was in the dressing room, getting ready for the night shift.

"Here you go, Elena. Carlo gave me these little pills that will make your tummy feel better. Come on now, hurry up so you can feel better soon."

"But I feel better already. I don't think I need the pills. Thank you anyway, Bea."

"Don't be silly, Elena. Carlo will be hurt if you refuse. Anyway, little pills like these can't hurt you. Come on, down the hatch!"

Elena did not have the energy to argue the point with her sister-in-law. She didn't feel comfortable with the situation, but reasoned that it would be childish to make a scene about some little white pills. She did find it odd, however, that as soon as she swallowed them, Bea grabbed the glass from her hand, and in a rush to get back to her room, nearly knocked Margot over in the hallway.

"Is everything all right, Mrs. Zimmerman?" Margot asked anxiously.

"Everything's fine, thank you. I just had a little tummy ache but I feel much better now."

"Good. Can I get you anything, Mrs. Zimmerman?"

"No, thank you, Margot. I'll just sit here awhile in my chair and watch some television. Why don't you relax in the other room till we order dinner?"

"Fine. But call me if you need anything. I'll leave the door open so I can hear you."

"You're so kind, Margot. You're all so kind. Thank you."

Those were the last words Margot would ever hear Elena say.

⁓

Margot was ready to go back to Elena's room and ask her what she would like to order for dinner when she heard cries coming from the bedroom.

Margot ran in and found Elena moaning in pain in her wheelchair.

"Mrs. Zimmerman, What's the matter? What happened?"

Elena, who was usually stoic, had her eyes closed in agony, while she clutched her midsection in distress. She couldn't form any words, she could only scream with pain as though something was tearing her insides apart.

Margot ran down the hall and banged with all her strength on the Manzianos' door. This time she would get them to answer even if she had to break it down.

Finally Margot heard the doors being unlocked. Carlo, all disheveled, stuck his head out to inquire, "What's all the commotion about? You're disturbing my wife. She's trying to take a nap."

"Please come quickly, Doctor. It's Mrs. Zimmerman. She's in an awful way, and in so much pain. I don't know what's wrong."

"Oh, all right, I'm coming. Just let me get my slippers on."

"Please hurry. I've never seen anyone suffer this way before."

When Carlo walked into Elena's room with the usual bland look on his face, Margot spoke up and said, "Dr. Manziano, don't you think we had better call Mrs. Zimmerman's doctor, or maybe 911? She probably should be in the hospital right now."

"Nonsense, Margot. I'll call a doctor I know and see what he says. Just wait here until I come back."

"Hurry, please hurry, Dr. Manziano. Maybe Mrs. Manziano could offer some support too."

"I don't think we'll bother my wife—you know that she's not well. I'll be right back."

Margot held Elena's trembling hand for twenty minutes until Carlo returned, with Bea at his side. He said, "I finally contacted the doctor. He's in the Hamptons right now and said that he would send one of his colleagues to cover the situation. In the meantime he said that we should give my sister a painkiller to ease her discomfort until the doctor arrives. I have some here we can give her. Will you get some water and see if you can get her to swallow one."

It took an hour for the doctor to arrive. Elena was still sitting in her wheelchair, moaning in pain, with Margo at her side. Carlo said to Margot, "This is Dr. Jonas. Would you wait outside?" But Margo, who was again holding Elena's hand, would not budge.

Dr. Jonas didn't bother to examine the patient, but after a meaningful nod from Bea, took out a syringe and gave Elena an injection. A few moments later, Elena lost consciousness and collapsed in her chair. Without any help from either doctor, Margot immediately picked Elena up as gently as she could, carried her in her arms, and laid her on the bed. Margot was relieved that Elena, in her unconsciousness, was at least freed from her pain.

"Thank you, Doctor," said Carlo, shaking the man's hand. "We'll let her rest tonight and call you tomorrow."

Margot was speechless as the doctor packed up his needles and syringes and left the room.

"No, Dr. Manziano," cried Margot. "Mrs. Zimmerman needs to go to the hospital right away. We have to call an ambulance. Mrs. Zimmerman might die tonight."

"No, no ambulance. That costs too much money. I know a cheaper way. It'll only take them about an hour to get here. I'll go call from my room. You stay with my sister."

As soon as he marched out of the room, Margot knew that Elena's fate, for better or for worse, was in her hands. Without a moment's hesitation, she picked up the phone and dialed 911. To Carlo and Bea's annoyance, the ambulance arrived within minutes. Margot no longer cared whether she had a job or not. She could not sit quietly by and let these people kill Mrs. Zimmerman.

Elena arrived at the hospital at approximately eight o'clock in the evening, with Margot still at her side. Carlo had reluctantly joined them in the ambulance, and when the doctor in charge asked him, "Does Mrs. Zimmerman have a Living Will?"

He answered, "No. But if her heart fails, do not resuscitate!" The doctor was momentarily taken aback, but was used to the many vagaries of human behavior in stressful situations.

—

At two o'clock the next afternoon, Jean-Paul's phone rang.

"Jean-Paul, it's Angelina. Gregorio and I are in California and just received a phone call from Carlo to say that Mummy was taken to the Emergency Room in Lenox Hill Hospital last night. He wasn't clear about the problem but said something vague about her heart. Would you do me a big favor and check on her? You can call me back at home."

"Of course, I'll go over right away. Only God knows what those two have done to her now. I'll call you later. 'Bye."

Within a half an hour he was in the Emergency Room telling the head nurse that he was there to see his mother. The young doctor who came over to question him seemed skeptical about his credentials and excused himself for a moment. He came back with a woman who looked at Jean-Paul with a quizzical look on her face.

The moment he said, "I'm Jean-Paul," the woman threw her arms around him and said, "I'm Margot, Mrs. Zimmerman's night aide. We've never met because you always come in the daytime. But I've heard so much about you. Mrs. Zimmerman loves you so much.

Marlene and Sheila are here too. They'll be so happy to see you."

That was enough validation for the doctor, who was immediately ready to escort him into Elena's cubicle.

"What exactly is my mother's problem, Doctor?"

"She was unconscious when she came in last night. It seems that she has a massive infection in her body and the most rigid abdomen I've ever seen in my professional life. As you know, she's eighty-seven years old, which complicates things. If she were a younger woman, we would be more aggressive in treating her. Right now we have her on life support."

"What are her chances of surviving this episode?"

The doctor looked Jean-Paul right in the eye and answered, "None!"

Jean-Paul was stunned for a moment and then said, "If it's of any help, I have her Living Will, of which I'm the executor."

"Thank God," said the doctor. "Her brother, Dr. Manziano, told us she didn't have one when she came in last night. But now we can give her life a compassionate ending."

"May I see my mother now, Doctor?"

"Of course, I'll take you there myself."

Since a private room was not yet available, the doctor and a nurse took Jean-Paul into a tiny cubicle with only a curtain to separate Elena from another patient—a woman in the middle of a serious cardiac episode.

The first thing he noticed were tubes—lots and lots of tubes—coming out of every part of Elena's body. But in spite of the swelling in her face, it was not hard to recognize his still-beautiful friend.

Elena was moaning softly and her eyes seemed swollen shut with pain. Jean-Paul had no way of knowing if she was conscious or not.

He walked around the bed and said, "Elena, it's me, Jean-Paul. Don't worry, we'll take good care of you now."

Jean-Paul gently stroked her forehead and asked the doctor, "Why does she seem to be suffering so? Can't you give her something for the pain?"

"We couldn't do that until we had the Living Will, since painkillers would affect her breathing and be counterproductive to the life support."

Jean-Paul really did not want to have a conversation about life support in front of Elena, so he led the doctor out of the room and said, "I trust you when you say that there is no hope for her to survive this episode. Therefore I give you the authority to take her off the life support and give her as much morphine as is necessary to stop her agony."

The doctor was very sympathetic, and within moments, Jean-Paul watched him gently remove the now-useless equipment that had been helping her deteriorating organs to function. It was painful to watch, since the process itself caused discomfort, especially when the breathing tubes were removed.

The nurse then came in to administer three injections to make Elena more comfortable.

The doctor, who had remained throughout the whole process, said in a low voice, "I can't predict how long it might be before she takes her last breath, but don't be surprised if she survives for no more than twenty minutes." Jean-Paul was as prepared as anyone can be under those circumstances.

Jean-Paul's immediate job was to call Angelina and Gregorio in California. He suspected that Angelina was not prepared to hear the truth and that it would be kinder if her son told his mother in the way he knew best. He was grateful that Gregorio was the one who answered the phone.

"Gregorio, it's me. Look, it's not good news. According to the doctor, your grandmother has a massive infection in her body and has no chance for survival. I just had them take her off of life support and give her morphine to ease the pain. He said that she might not even last through the next twenty minutes. I'm so sorry. I promise I'll keep you informed all the way. Give your mother my love and tell her that Elena is resting peacefully. You can also say that I'm not leaving until it's over."

"Thank you, Jean-Paul. I'll tell her. And call at any hour of the night."

Jean-Paul then returned to Elena's tiny cubicle, where he was able to sit with her for the next couple of hours. She seemed to be at peace as he held her hand and caressed her forehead.

He said, "I hope you know how much you're loved. You've done your work well and now you can rest peacefully. You're loved unconditionally."

Elena's "son" didn't know how many of his words she actually heard (although it is said that hearing is the last of our senses to go), but he was sure that on some level of her consciousness she understood every word he said.

At 5:00 p.m. Jean-Paul went outside the Emergency Room to call his partner, Christopher, who was planning to leave for London that night.

"Christopher, I have some difficult news to tell you. No, I'm all right. It's Elena. She's in the Emergency Room. It doesn't look good."

"Thank God I just canceled my flight to London for tonight. I canceled it a few minutes ago for reasons I can't explain. I just had an uneasy feeling that I shouldn't go. I'll join you in a few minutes. You're sure you're okay?"

"Yeah, just tell them you're her son. It'll save you a lot of trouble. See you in a bit."

On his way back to Elena's room, the doctor stopped him to reiterate that there was no telling how long Elena would last.

Jean-Paul took the opportunity to ask the young doctor, "You know who Mrs. Zimmerman is, don't you?"

"No, I don't think I do. Who is she?"

"You're a young man and it's been a long time since her face graced the pages of magazines and newspapers, but have you ever heard of Zimmerman Investments, Incorporated? Elena is the widow of the Philip Zimmerman, the man who owned all of that."

"Wow! Wait till I tell my wife. Do you mean that this is the Elena Zimmerman?"

Jean-Paul was not just tooting Elena's horn for no apparent reason. He knew the value and benefits that could sometimes be obtained for a high profile patient.

When he entered Elena's room, Marlene and Sheila were huddled in the only two chairs that fit into the tiny space. Although Carlo and Bea had made life nearly impossible for them, Elena had always been more than generous to all the loving people around her, and they were not going to abandon her now.

The women offered him a seat, but he preferred to stand next to the bed, where he could hold Elena's hand. He had just begun to wonder about Carlo and Bea and where they could possibly be hiding while Elena was on her deathbed. It was 6:00 p.m. when Carlo walked into the room. He had left his sister alone since the day before. And there was still no sign of Bea.

The sight of the dreaded Dr. Manziano finally caused the two faithful women to take their leave and wait in the hall. Moments later, Christopher came in. He kissed Elena, who, at eighty-seven years of age, looked like Sleeping Beauty, and got an update from Jean-Paul as to her condition. Carlo never asked.

While the three of them were taking turns sitting in the two available chairs, the nurse came in and said,

"A private room down the hall just became available. The doctor says that, if you want, we can move Mrs. Zimmerman in there, so you can all sit comfortably. Besides which, we won't have to ask you to leave after a certain hour."

Carlo then turned to the nurse, gave a nervous laugh, and said, "That won't be necessary. She's not going to last much longer!"

The nurse, taken aback, answered, "Well, you're certainly pragmatic!"

Jean-Paul and Christopher, who understood that Carlo was only afraid that a private room in the Emergency Department might cost a few more dollars, quickly overruled him and said in unison, "We'll take it!"

After the staff had moved Elena into the new room, everyone but Carlo recognized it as a godsend for their friend's last hours of life. It was bright and functional, with enough chairs for Jean-Paul, Christopher, Sheila, Marlene, and, of course, the "pragmatic" Carlo. The new space was also quiet. The only sound was of Elena's shallow breathing behind the oxygen mask.

Jean-Paul sat next to Elena, on her right side, and continued to hold her hand. And when the air conditioning got a bit chilly, he raised the blanket up over her shoulders. He paid little attention to the quiet conversation around him, but his heart nearly stopped beating when he heard Sheila say, "Jean-Paul was the love of Mrs. Zimmerman's life." It was a tribute he would never forget.

Carlo just sat there the whole time, shaking his head and letting it periodically drop. He seemed far away, lost in his own world. The others in the room felt free to speak any way they wished, since they knew that he was probably too deaf to understand anything they said.

By eight o'clock Marlene and Sheila said their good-byes to everyone, including Elena. They both had husbands and children waiting for them at home. They knew that Elena would be all right as long as Jean-Paul and Christopher were with her.

There was not much conversation in the room after the two women had left. From time to time, either Christopher or Jean-Paul would say, "Remember when…" and talk about the good times and the countless laughs that they had shared with Elena. But mostly, they found themselves taking each breath with Elena and praying that, for her sake, it would soon be over.

As the hours ticked by, Jean-Paul and Christopher marveled at the way Elena's skin had stayed so young.

"Christopher, look at how smooth her hands are. That's something no surgeon can manufacture. It's almost impossible to believe that she's eighty-seven years old. Even with no makeup and her hair pulled back, you can still see the five-year-old girl who sat on her parents' porch, smiling at the passers-by who stopped to admire the beautiful child."

By midnight, Elena would occasionally stop breathing for a moment. Then, after a few seconds, she would make a great effort to take a deeper breath than before. Although she was not ready to give up yet, her demeanor became increasingly peaceful as the hours droned by.

Finally, at 3:05 a.m., Elena took her last breath. It was over. Jean-Paul had stayed at her side for twelve and a half hours and Christopher had been there for eight and a half.

A few moments after Elena had passed on, Jean-Paul and Christopher were both aware that the body of the woman they had known and loved was now an empty shell. As Jean-Paul's tears spilled onto Elena when he kissed her goodbye, he could feel the room filling up with her vibrant spirit. He could almost touch it. She seemed to be reaching out to him and Christopher and saying, "It's all right. I'm fine now and I will love you forever."

Christopher, who had never known Elena before the damage to the motor portion of her brain, put his arm around Jean-Paul, held him close, and said, "She's young and beautiful again."

On their way home through the empty streets of New York, Jean-Paul thought back to the last time he had seen Elena in her lonely, barren bedroom. Before leaving, he had said, "One of the most inspiring things about you, Elena, is that you've taught me to be unfailingly generous to everyone I meet."

"Thank you, Jean-Paul. I remember so well the thirteen-year-old boy who walked into our lives the night of Angelina's thirteenth birthday party, and I am so proud of the man that you have become."

—

The moment Elena took her last breath, Carlo did not even bother to pretend to say goodbye to his sister. He just disappeared. When Jean-Paul left the room to tell the doctor that Mrs. Zimmerman had passed on, he saw Carlo on his cell phone, talking to Bea, laughing and smiling. He was ninety-one and Bea was eighty-seven. They had waited thirty-five-years for this moment.

Little did they know that things might not turn out exactly the way they had planned.

CHAPTER 22

"Bea, I'm home," Carlo called out as he entered the apartment, about half an hour after Elena died. He immediately noticed that something was different, but he couldn't quite figure out what it was. It finally dawned on him that it was the first time in years that not only were all the doors open, but the lights were on.

"I'm back here," cried out Bea, "just checking on what's left in her room now that she's gone."

When Carlo reached Elena's bedroom, he saw Bea dressed up in Elena's favorite black velvet Valentino evening gown. She had adorned her face with some garish makeup and wound her long white hair around her head. A half-empty bottle of Moet Chandon was on the coffee table, and Bea cradled a tall thin Baccarat champagne glass in her hands. It was almost four o'clock in the morning, and eighty-seven-year old Bea was in a party mood.

"Bea, I've had a long night and I'm tired. Could we please just go to bed? We have lots of things to attend to tomorrow."

"Not as much as you think! I already started clearing out anything valuable that was still in her room. You'll notice that the miniature Louis XV chest of drawers is gone. And if you look at the walls, you'll see that the Marc Chagall painting has been removed. Of course, I couldn't take away all of the porcelain de Sévres in the living room, since I imagine that Angelina and her brat will be coming to bury Elena, but I've managed to take certain pieces away. We can always hide them in the basement or put them in a locked closet with the rest. They don't have to know about the storage downstairs, and as far as they're concerned, the locked closets are filled with our clothes. Simple! Now, how about some champagne?"

"But, Bea, we don't know when they'll be coming to New York. I haven't even called Angelina yet to say that her mother is dead."

"Oh fiddle-faddle. That sissy boy Jean-Paul has probably already told them. You can always call them in the morning and see when they're arriving. And don't forget, no giggling on the phone. You have to sound appropriately saddened by your loss. However, we have to know how much time we have left to finish clearing out the good stuff."

"Yes, Bea, I'll do that first thing tomorrow, but now I really need to get some rest. I'm ninety-one years old and I can't take these late nights the way I used to."

"You go ahead and sleep, old man, while I sit here and enjoy the fruits of our labor."

Carlo no longer had the energy to do more than shake his head back and forth all the way to his urine-soaked couch that he slept on every night.

—

"Gregorio, this is Carlo. Your grandmother died last night. When are you and your mother coming to New York?" Carlo asked in a cold and abrupt manner. It was as though he had completely disconnected from the human race.

"Yes, Carlo, Jean-Paul and Christopher called last night, and we're flying in tomorrow. We should arrive sometime in the afternoon."

"We'll be here," said Carlo, abruptly terminating the conversation.

A few minutes later, he dialed Jean-Paul's number and said, "Jean-Paul, this is Carlo. I can't remember. When are Angelina and Gregorio arriving in New York?"

"Tomorrow afternoon, Carlo."

Jean-Paul had barely heard him say "Okay" when Carlo had, in his usual charming way, hung up the phone.

"Bea, they'll be here tomorrow. We have lots to do before they get here."

"Don't worry. I already hid most of the valuables. Look, the little Renoir that she loved so much is stuffed amongst a pile of papers on your air-conditioner. No one would think of looking there! I did lots of work while you were sitting on your ass in the hospital waiting for your precious sister to take her last breath. We can tell Angelina and Gregorio that the packing boxes in all the rooms are personal items that we plan to send to California."

"I don't know, Bea. It all looks pretty funny to me."

"Oh, you stupid, stupid man! We haven't come this far for nothing. Now let's open that last bottle of champagne before those two get here. Ha! Wait until they see the document leaving us the Zimmerman Trust!"

In the meantime, knowing that Carlo and Bea would never bother with funeral arrangements, Angelina called Jean-Paul and asked, "Jean-Paul, we know that Carlo is not capable of tying his own shoelaces, so would you mind asking Campbell's Funeral Home to pick up my mother's body from the hospital? You can tell them that we'll make further arrangements after we arrive."

"Of course, Angie, no problem. By the way, that idiot uncle of yours just called me to verify when you're arriving. I don't think that the two of them want any surprises. But I want you and Gregorio to be prepared for a shock when you see the condition of your mother's apartment—and not just the filth. Call me when you get in, okay?"

"Okay, and thank you for being there with Mother till the end. We'll see you soon."

Angelina and Gregorio had a hard time not showing the shock they felt when they first entered Elena's apartment, which had once been so immaculately kept. Every piece of furniture was covered in filth. Nothing had been cleaned in years, and each room was filled with packing cases.

First Gregorio called Marlene and Margot and asked, "I know Mrs. Zimmerman is gone, but do you think that you could help us to make some sense out of all this chaos? If you don't have another job yet, we'd love to hire you for the next couple of weeks."

Both women said that they would be more than happy to come and do whatever they could to clear up some of the mess. They were also curious to find out how Elena's daughter and grandson were going to deal with the dreaded Manzianos.

As Angelina and Gregorio walked through the apartment, Angelina whispered, "What on earth happened to all of Mummy's things? Even most of her clothes are missing. Gregorio, please call Mr. Haimoff and tell him that we need to set up a meeting right away."

Angelina then called Jean-Paul and said, "I know Mummy is at Campbell's Funeral Home. Do you think that you could make an appointment for us to go and talk to them tomorrow morning?"

"Sure, Angie, that's no problem. I'll make it for sometime around ten o'clock so that you don't have to rush in the morning."

"Will you and Christopher come with Gregorio and me?"

"Have we ever not been there for each other?"

"Okay, just come to the house first and we'll go together."

Jean-Paul knew how traumatic the situation was for his old friend. When Angelina's husband had died, she had him cremated, according to his wishes, and sent the remains to Jean-Paul in New York. It was too painful for her to see them or have them near her. Angelina also knew that Jean-Paul already had Helen Dawson's cremated remains in his home, so he would have no problem safeguarding one more urn. And Angelina was well aware that, within a short period of time, she would be joining her late husband. Then Gregorio could bury them together.

The next morning, a director at Campbell's Funeral Home asked Angelina, Gregorio, Jean-Paul, and Christopher if they wanted to view the body.

The director said, "It's customary, when someone dies in the hospital, for the funeral home to have a family member identify the deceased and make sure that there was no mix-up along the way."

Angelina immediately declined the offer to see her mother, so Jean-Paul, Christopher, and Gregorio left her in one of the offices while they went into the chapel where Elena was laid out.

Elena seemed so peaceful and young, as though she might wake up at any moment, laugh at their serious expressions, and get up and leave with them.

It was when Jean-Paul reached down to caress her forehead that he felt the cold chill of the refrigerated drawer she had been placed in, in order to preserve what was left of her mortal body. He knew in an instant that it was real—his beloved Elena was truly gone from this earthly plane forever. He would never hear her raucous laugh or her words of love and encouragement again. He would miss her terribly, but he was relieved to know that she was finally at peace.

After they vouched that it was truly Elena's body, Angelina joined them and they were taken into another room to choose an appropriate urn for her cremated remains. None of them found anything that they felt was right for the Elena they had all known and loved, so they went back to the apartment to search for a container that they thought Elena would approve of.

In Elena's bedroom they discovered an antique carved ivory and wood box that Carlo and Bea must have overlooked in their zealous search for all the precious items in the room. It had been sitting unobtrusively in front of the fireplace, partially hidden by a chair— almost as though Elena herself had hidden it from them for just this purpose.

"This is perfect," said the four in unison.

"If you want, Christopher and I can take it back to Campbell's for you this afternoon," offered Jean-Paul.

"Thank you. That would be great, since Gregorio and I have a meeting with the lawyer this afternoon."

When Jean-Paul and Christopher attempted to hand over the antique ivory and wood box to the funeral director, he asked them to take it back home. "It would be better if we send you Mrs. Zimmerman's cremated remains. You can then put them in the box yourselves," said the man.

The box was too valuable for the funeral home to keep on the premises.

~

That afternoon, Angelina and Gregorio were in Harry Haimoff's office with the will that they had pried out from under Elena's dressing table.

"We're so glad to meet you, Mr. Haimoff. You were so wonderful to my mother. Thank God for Helen Dawson, or she would never have been protected at all," said Angelina.

"First of all, please call me Harry."

Gregorio took over for his mother, and said, "One of the problems, Harry, is that two of my grandmothers' aides came to the apartment early this morning and were shocked that most of the paintings and works of art which were in place when she went to the hospital are now gone. We can only imagine what my mother's aunt and uncle have done with them in the last forty-eight hours. But you should see the apartment. There are dozens of packing boxes in every room and all of the closets have been locked. Carlo and Bea say that they're filled with their personal belongings.

"By the way, we told the aides to go home today because we didn't want them being harassed by the Manzianos when we're not there."

Harry Haimoff was not sitting in a beautiful office filled with fine paintings and antiques for being the dullest knife in the drawer. He had earned his position by being one of the shrewdest lawyers in the business. He also worked fast—before people like Carlo and Bea would know what hit them.

"First of all we have to make a thorough search of the apartment, including the storage rooms in the basement. Then we have to get in touch with the banks and find out where the money has gone. I'm sure that the Zimmerman Trust is intact, but we need to know what happened to the income and to anything they might have sold."

Although Harry Haimoff was first and foremost a lawyer, he had not been immune to Elena's charm, and he welcomed the task of protecting her daughter and grandson.

Harry, Angelina, and Gregorio immediately went back to Elena's apartment to try to get some answers from Carlo and Bea. The couple practically had to be pried out of their rooms.

Harry introduced himself in a non-threatening manner and casually mentioned, "I must say, I'm surprised that some of the artwork that Mrs. Zimmerman bequeathed to the museum is not in the apartment. Do you know where it might be at this time?"

As usual, Carlo and Bea disavowed any knowledge about Mrs. Zimmerman's property that had disappeared. Haimoff asked about specific paintings and precious objects, but the two oldsters remained silent.

Gregorio, having heard about the frenzy that Elena's Living Will had caused, thought it was strange that they did not react at all to the news that Elena had made a new will that they had known nothing about. And it was even more bizarre that neither of them asked to see it.

"What about the closets, Dr. Manziano?" asked Harry in a cool and collected voice. "I can see that they're locked. Do you think you could give us the keys? And do you also have the keys for the storage rooms in the basement?"

Carlo stammered, "I don't know where the keys are, but all you'll find in there are our clothes. As for the storage in the basement, there's only one room. I don't know where the key is right now, but we'll look for it later. We haven't been down there in years."

Harry was well aware that the best thing to do now was send the Manzianos back to their quarters while he, Angelina and Gregorio did some investigating.

Their first stop was the basement, where they encountered the Superintendent of the building—another person who had no use for Carlo and Bea. He knew very well that the Christmas bonuses had secretly come from Elena and not from her brother and sister-in-law. All that the building staff had ever received from the Manzianos were rude demands and no tips—two things that did not endear them to anyone. The stupidity of such behavior is that you never know when the very same people you treated badly will find the opportunity to get their revenge.

When the Superintendent heard that Dr. Manziano had no key to the storage room, he said, "But Mr. Haimoff, he is constantly running back and forth from the apartment to the basement with armloads of packages. He even took a second storage bin recently. Actually, there has been more activity than usual in the last couple of days. Come with me. I can show you where they are and have one of the men break the locks for Mrs. Zimmerman's daughter and grandson."

Harry said, "I think we should start with the storage bin that has been the busiest since Mrs. Zimmerman went to the hospital."

"No problem. Hey Pete, get the cutters to open the Zimmerman storage, please."

Within a few minutes they were surrounded by box upon box of everything one could imagine.

"Look over here," said Gregorio to his mother and Harry. "It's a garbage bag with the Chagall painting that disappeared from Lolo's room while she was in the hospital."

"Can you believe the pieces of porcelain de Sévres hidden amongst those old frying pans?" cried out Angelina in horror and disgust.

"All right," said Harry, "we don't have to go any further for the moment. Let's put new locks on the two storage rooms so no one else can get in. I'll go back to the office now and see how my associates are doing with our investigation of the Zimmerman Trust and bank accounts. We're doing a full investigation of Mrs. Zimmerman's accounts, as well as the ones that belong to the Manzianos. I have a feeling that the activity between them should be quite interesting."

"One more thing before you go, Harry," said Angelina. "You may not know this, but I don't really know how long I have to live. I've already beaten all of the odds, but it can't go on forever. Therefore, I wonder if there's a way that we can bypass me as the inheritor and make my son the heir? It wouldn't make sense to pay inheritance taxes twice in a possibly short period of time."

"Of course, my dear, it can all be arranged quite easily. Just let me get the paperwork started. Now let's go back upstairs and see if those two will open the closets for us. In any case, we're going to have to hire security guards to make sure that the Manzianos don't leave the apartment with any packages that don't belong to them. For now, I suggest that we all stay calm and friendly so as not to alarm them unduly. We can scare them a bit, but they must not know the extent of the inquiries we are making before we have enough evidence to throw the book at them."

⁓

There was plenty of work to be done just cleaning the apartment, and Angelina went at it with a vengeance.

She couldn't bear to see the elegant home that Elena had been so proud of, reduced to a rubbish heap.

She said to Jean-Paul on the phone, "I don't know why I'm doing this. I'm a dying woman." But still she worked on, with Marlene and Margot at her side.

After a couple of days, Carlo and Bea, who had stayed cooped up in their quarters, went to Angelina and Gregorio with a document in hand. It was the paper that the aides had witnessed without being shown what they were signing. In essence, it said that Elena was leaving the Zimmerman Trust to her brother and sister-in-law, and it was signed five days before Elena died.

When the lawyer showed the document to Marlene and Margot, who had suffered much abuse from the Manzianos, they were more than happy to say, "Yes, we signed a paper, but Mrs. Manziano would not allow us to see what it said. Everything but the place we were expected to sign was covered up by a piece of paper. Furthermore, Mrs. Zimmerman could not have signed her name to it, since she lost the use of her right hand back in 2001. We even wrote the notes and cards that she sent to Jean-Paul and Christopher."

At this point, Carlo and Bea must have known that they might have gone a bit too far. Suddenly, objects such as the miniature Louis XV chest of drawers began to miraculously reappear in the apartment. But the Manzianos still refused to acknowledge that they knew anything about the missing items that had been bequeathed to the museum, or how other things had rematerialized in the apartment. And there were still many precious objects unaccounted for.

At one point, Bea went to Angelina, who was cleaning her mother's bathroom, attempting to take years of grime off of every fixture, so she could feel comfortable using them.

"Angelina, I know that you and Gregorio are planning to sell your mother's apartment, but do you think that Carlo and I could stay on for another ten months? You see, your uncle and I sold our house in California so that we could afford to stay here and take care of your mother."

"You couldn't afford to keep your house in California?" answered Angelina. "What about the twenty-five thousand dollars a month you and Carlo took as a salary? Neither you nor your husband ever paid a bill for the last thirty-five years. Not to mention that you never paid taxes, either."

After that, Angelina bit her lip so as not to tip off the Manzianos that the powers that be were rapidly uncovering tons of incriminating evidence against them.

The next day, in direct contradiction to what she had said the day before, Bea threw her nose up in the air and told Gregorio, "You can tell your mother that we certainly don't need to stay here longer than necessary. After all, our home in California is just as nice as this apartment, if not nicer!"

That may be so, but it can't be more cluttered or covered in filth, thought Gregorio, as Bea stormed out of the room.

—

The last week of May, about two weeks after Elena's death, Harry Haimoff phoned Gregorio. "Gregorio, this is Harry. Are you able to speak freely on the phone right now?"

"I certainly am, Harry. Carlo and Bea spend most of the time locked in their rooms. What's going on?"

"I'd like to set up a face-to-face meeting with the Manzianos. It should be as soon as possible. Right now we need to safeguard what valuables may still be hidden away in the apartment or in the Manzianos' quarters."

"How about tomorrow afternoon at two o'clock? Would that suit you?"

"That would be fine. Just make sure that Carlo and Bea are there with you and your mother. We can all sit in the living room with the doors shut. There's no need for anyone else to be a witness to the showdown."

"I'll see that everyone is there on time, even if I have to break down their door!"

That night Angelina and Gregorio couldn't help but feel some apprehension over the next day's confrontation. It would not be easy for them to deal with their elderly relatives, but they had to remember that the old crooks had plotted every move and had stolen and lied for decades.

CHAPTER 23

The next afternoon, Carlo and Bea showed up in the living room at exactly two o'clock. Harry, Angelina, and Gregorio were already seated on one of the two blue silk sofas, which faced each other in front of the fireplace. It was the coziest spot in the massive room. Although the porcelain de Sévres, or what was left of it, was in vitrines on either side of the fireplace, there was a large empty space over the fireplace where the Ingres painting had previously been hung.

As soon as the Manzianos were comfortably seated, Harry began to speak—again in a non-confrontational way. He deemed it wise to keep them off their guard for as long as possible.

"Dr. and Mrs. Manziano, thank you for coming today. There are a few things we need to clear up about Mrs. Zimmerman's finances and works of art. I wonder if you could tell us, Doctor, how much Mrs. Zimmerman had in the Zimmerman Trust?"

"I'm not quite sure without the papers in front of me, but I would say, between three and four million dollars."

"Oh, Dr. Manziano, I'm afraid that you're mistaken. According to our information, it's more in the neighborhood of one hundred million dollars."

He reached down into his briefcase and brought out a sheaf of papers, which he calmly rested in his lap. He took one quick glance at the sheet on top and said, "Hmm, yes, a little over a hundred million.

"Now, about the artwork that belonged to Mrs. Zimmerman. Why don't we start with the painting by Chagall that used to hang in her bedroom? Would you by any chance know where it is today?"

"We have no knowledge of those things. Some of them were sold at Mrs. Zimmerman's request in order to pay the bills."

"But Doctor Manziano, why should Mrs. Zimmerman have to sell any of the art, especially the pieces that she willed to the museum, if there was one hundred million dollars in her Trust? After all, she rarely left the house, no longer bought any clothes for herself, and didn't even have her makeup man and hairdresser come to the house every day, the way she used to."

Harry then reached down next to the sofa and pulled out a large flat object wrapped in a garbage bag. He extracted the Chagall that he, Angelina, and Gregorio had found in the basement storage bin—the one Carlo had sworn didn't exist.

"Does this look like the Chagall, Doctor?"

"I have no idea where that came from," stammered Carlo.

For once, Bea was quiet as a mouse. She was going to wait and see how this game would play out.

"Now, Doctor, am I correct in the assumption that you had the late Mrs. Zimmerman's power of attorney, and therefore paid all of her bills?"

"Yeah, I did."

"Then please tell me why it was necessary for you to transfer fifty thousand dollars from her account to yours after she had passed away? You know that once a person has died, the power of attorney automatically becomes invalid."

"Well, uhhm, we have some storage bills to pay in California each month."

"Fifty thousand dollars for storage? That's an exorbitant amount of money. And shouldn't you be paying some of your bills out of the twenty-five thousand dollars a month you've been receiving all these years?"

Harry quickly continued, "But let's not quibble about fifty thousand dollars. Let's get down to brass tacks about the transfers of large sums of money—again from your late sister's accounts to yours. I have here the documents indicating how much money you transferred to your account since Mrs. Zimmerman gave you her power of attorney when she became too incapacitated to sign anything herself. I believe it amounts to at least ten million dollars. Am I correct?

"You wrote out checks for up to four hundred and fifty thousand dollars at a time, while your sister was made to live without even the basic necessities. You not only took millions of dollars in cash for yourself, but we have copies of the checks from the sales at Sotheby's and Christie's which were made out to you for Mrs. Zimmerman's works of art. How or why you thought you had the right to do it is beyond my comprehension, especially since your sister was an unusually generous woman who had always taken good care of her family."

By this time, Bea was ready to explode. Her carefully executed plans had just gone terribly wrong, and she had no intention of being the one to pay the piper.

Bea took one leap off the couch, looked down at her husband and, as they say, threw him under the bus.

"You stupid, stupid man! How could you do such a monstrous thing to your own sister? I'm appalled!"

After getting that off her chest, she marched over to a chair in a corner of the room, sat down, and looked at Carlo as though she had just discovered that Adolph Hitler had been sitting next to her.

Harry calmly looked over at Bea and stopped her dead in her tracks. "But, Mrs. Manziano, you have to understand that you are as culpable as your husband, since half of the money was transferred to your account as well."

The game was over. Carlo was just confused, but Bea understood that it was up to her to try and minimize the danger for both of them.

Her first question was, "How much do we owe?"

Then, in a self-serving plea for compassion, she said, "I don't want my husband to go to jail."

"Do you think we could have access to some of your paperwork concerning the state of Mrs. Zimmerman's affairs? It may be that you were not properly informed. May we go to your study now, Doctor, and see what you can show us?" asked Harry, in an effort to appease the elderly couple and gain admission into their private quarters.

Carlo and Bea knew they were at a distinct disadvantage. There was no way that they could refuse a polite request to see some papers, which were in a state of such chaos that even they could no longer make any sense of them. They could still hope that, with enough cooperation, they might get away without being prosecuted. After all, Angelina and Gregorio were still family.

Bea stayed in the living room with Angelina while Harry and Gregorio followed Carlo into his study.

The first thing that the lawyer and Gregorio noticed was the overwhelming smell of urine that permeated the office. There was a desk at one end, piled high with papers and old letters, and against one wall was a white couch with a rumpled grey cashmere blanket on it. As they came closer, it became evident that the smell of stale urine came from the couch. Two of the walls, which were covered in a rich, shiny red leather, had ceiling-to-floor metal and glass bookcases filled with numerous books and piles of papers. Packing boxes filled the rest of the office.

Making their way across this sea of confusion was not easy. Gregorio soon felt nauseated from the overpowering smell of urine. When he moved around the desk to open a window lest he pass out or throw up on the musty carpet, he accidentally dislodged the papers on the air conditioner. Bending down to pick them up, he perceived the corner of a picture frame sticking out of the mess.

"Don't bother with those things," said Carlo.

"I'm sorry, I was just clumsy and knocked them over while attempting to get some air into the room.… Hey, what's this? It looks like the Renoir that my grandmother always had in her room. Well, what do you know? It is her Renoir. What is it doing in the middle of these files? Harry, look at this. We found Lolo's little Renoir!"

"I don't know how that got in there. I've never seen it before," Carlo insisted.

Harry, who had also had enough of the putrid room, decided it was time to put an end to the charade.

"Dr. Manziano, I think the time has come to lay our cards on the table. Let's go back and join the ladies in the living room while we discuss where we all go from here."

⁓

When everyone was once again seated in the living room, Harry answered Bea's earlier question, "How much do we owe?"

"Mrs. Manziano, here is a copy of the transfers to your husband's accounts and to your accounts. We fully expect each of you to return these funds within three days.

"It would also be advisable for you and your husband to make arrangements to return to your home in California as soon as possible. Shall we agree on two weeks from today, so we can have a cleaning crew come in the week after? As you may know, Mrs. Zimmerman's principal heirs wish to sell the apartment as soon as possible.

"We're going to need a certain amount of time to go through every packing box in the house before you go, so that we can determine what is your personal property and what belongs to Mrs. Zimmerman's estate.

"You must also know that, after today, there will be a security guard stationed at the front and back entrances to the apartment. Neither of you will be allowed to leave without being searched. And any package you have with you will be opened and inspected as well.

"I think that about covers everything for the moment. I think that we understand each other. You know that your niece and her son do not wish you any harm, but the games are over.

"Now, Angelina, if you and Gregorio have a moment, there are a few things that we need to discuss."

"Does that mean that Carlo and I are free to go now?"

"Certainly, Mrs. Manziano. We'll be in touch later. And don't forget, we expect the funds to be returned within three days. Thank you!"

Carlo and Bea ran back to the safety of their rooms as fast as they could.

Meanwhile, Harry had a few points to make to Angelina and Gregorio.

"I think that went very well, under the circumstances. I don't know how much the Doctor understands or how in touch with reality either of them is, but I can only counsel you that it would be inadvisable to prosecute a ninety-one-year-old man and his eighty-seven-year-old wife. No judge or jury would ask for anything more than the return of property.

"The important thing now is to send these people back to California as quickly as we can, and to sell the apartment so the two of you can go on with your lives. Just leave the inheritance problems to me. That's my job.

"Angelina, we have already started the process of bypassing you in favor of your son, who, I'm sure, will make you proud."

—

After the confrontation with Harry, Angelina, and Gregorio in the living room, Carlo and Bea had returned to their rooms and, as always, locked the doors behind them.

Carlo sat down quietly on the sea of urine that covered the couch in his study and shook his head from side to side the way he usually did when his brain was trying to sort out a confusing issue.

It did not help his thought process to have Bea standing over him, jabbering, "You stupid, stupid man. I have to do everything around here. All you can do is sit on that smelly couch, looking foolish. I tell you, they're not getting the best of me!"

"I have an idea. After we give them back some of the money they say that we owe them, and go back to California for a while, we should buy a similar apartment in this building for ourselves. That'll show them who they're dealing with. Are you listening, Carlo? I said, are you listening to me?"

"Yes, dear. I'm listening. That's very good. But now we have to return the money we owe to the estate."

"That's your affair, not mine. We can leave some of our things here so that we have them when we move back into the building."

Since the confrontation in the living room, Bea could not accept that they had lost the battle, and had convinced herself that she could afford a thirty-million-dollar apartment.

She added, "You take care of the business and send our packing boxes to the house in Los Angeles. I only hope there's room, since we've sent so many of them over the years. We have at least a couple of weeks to get ready. The house in California can store our packing boxes and we can furnish our apartment here with some of the furniture from this apartment. They at least owe us that much. Then our lives will really begin."

Carlo had learned, over the years, that it was always best to agree with his wife—even when he couldn't hear what she was saying.

Despite the Manzianos' reluctance, the ten million dollars that they had pilfered was transferred back into Elena's account within the required three days.

Harry Haimoff and his crew found that most of the packing boxes and closets were filled with useless junk that Bea was hoarding. However, every time a precious object came to light in the midst of the confusion, it was hard to believe that there was not some method to her madness.

When the time came for the Manzianos to leave, Gregorio had to make the plane reservations, since Carlo couldn't figure out how it was done. One of Harry's associates would even accompany the couple to the airport, to make sure they got on the plane. The last thing the Manzianos took with them was a large briefcase filled with cash. No one was fooled when Carlo and Bea told them that it contained important documents, but Angelina and Gregorio figured that another couple hundred thousand dollars in cash was well worth the price of getting them out of the apartment with a minimum of fuss.

Now, since Gregorio and Harry had already been in Carlo's office, the next step would be to tackle Bea's bedroom, which she had obsessively kept under lock and key for so many years.

CHAPTER 24

Once Carlo and Bea had left for the airport, Harry Haimoff said to Angelina and Gregorio, "All of the Manzianos' bags and packing boxes were checked by our security before they left, so we know that nothing of value is missing—that is, unless they sent it to California before you both arrived. Come on, let's see what we find in Bea's bedroom."

Although Angelina had been expecting the worst, nothing could have prepared her for the sight or smell of Bea's bedroom—if one could still call it that.

"It's not possible. No sane person could live in this environment. And the musty smell of old, unwashed clothes and dirty bed linen is more than one can bear," cried Angelina.

And the smell was only the beginning.

The most prominent piece of furniture in the room was a large four-poster bed, piled four feet high with dirty clothes and old rags. Angelina went over to a tiny open space on the bed and said, "Not only is there hardly enough room for a child to lie down, but the sheets are so dirty that I can't tell what the original color was. And whew, I don't even want to touch the things on top. They're so dirty that they stink up the whole place. No wonder she never allowed anyone in here. My God, how many boxes are scattered around the room? There must be enough to fill every closet in the apartment. I think we're going to need rubber gloves to go through this chaos."

"Maybe you'd better not look in the bathroom, Mother. The tub, sink and toilet are black with dirt. And the floor is even worse. I don't think the towels have been cleaned in years. Tell me, Harry, how come my grandmother had to pay a dry cleaning bill of two thousand dollars for Carlo and Bea every month, while they lived like this?"

"Gregorio, look at this. It's one of Mummy's beautiful silk Japanese kimonos that she bought in Tokyo, thrown in a heap in the corner. It looks as though someone has taken a pair of shears and torn it to ribbons. This is getting more disturbing by the minute."

Harry, who had seen many bizarre cases of human behavior in his long career, tried to calm Angelina and Gregorio as best he could, while still preparing them for the possibility of more hidden atrocities. "Now don't get yourselves too upset over this room, kids. We've only started, and there may be plenty more surprises in store for us."

Gregorio soon discovered that opening the closets was a perilous undertaking—if he didn't open them with caution, he might suddenly find himself buried under an avalanche of unimaginable stuff.

The main closet across from the bed was particularly disturbing for Angelina. In it she found not only Elena's old underclothes and stockings, mixed in with some of her old nightgowns, probably taken out of the trash, but also the brand new nightgowns that Elena had requested.

"Gregorio, look, on the top shelf. There's Mummy's David Webb jewelry that Carlo and Bea insisted that she sell after they had convinced her that she was poor. She loved those pieces so much, especially this Jaguar bracelet. I remember Daddy not wanting to buy them because he only wanted her to have jewels with the value built into the size of the stones. But he bought them anyway, because he knew they made her happy. To think that they should end up in this pigsty. My God, there are more of Mummy's belongings in this room than Bea's! She was hoarding everything of my mother's as though they were hers. How creepy can you get? I wonder how many more of Mummy's things ended up at their house in California over the years."

They knew it would take days for them to clear out all the rooms in the apartment. Angelina put on a pair of rubber gloves and started on Bea's bathroom, while Gregorio tackled the closets and packing boxes. Meanwhile, Harry checked out the paperwork that the couple had left in Carlo's office.

Angelina had taken on the most distasteful task of all. But before scrubbing the murky mess in the bathroom, she started clearing out the drawers in the vanity.

"Gregorio, come quick. What is the Zimmerman vermeil silverware doing in a bathroom drawer, mixed in with dozens of Mummy's empty pill bottles? And this drawer is filled with empty soapboxes, more old prescription bottles, and used toothbrushes. The bottom one is filled to the brim with the wrappers of Maxi-Thin pantyliner pads. Yuk! Maybe I'll find the used pads in another drawer. What kind of a person keeps dozens of useless containers? I can't do any more of this right now. This is too gross. Tomorrow we can throw out Bea's trash. Now let's go see what Harry's doing."

Angelina and Gregorio found the lawyer sitting at the desk in Carlo's room, sorting out the papers he deemed important. It was slow going, since he never knew what piece of art he might discover next among the ruins, or what random piece of paper might be of use in the closing of the estate.

"Come here, kids, and get a look at this. It appears to me that Carlo kept all of Elena's mail in his desk, most of it unopened. I see here a letter dated years ago, from a Mr. Lane informing Mrs. Zimmerman that his wife, Lynn, who at one time had been married to your Uncle Angelo, passed away of a liver disease. Do you know if he ever passed the news on to Elena?"

"No, never," answered Angelina, "She would certainly have told me about it. Poor Lynn, she never had much of a chance. Mummy was always afraid that all that vodka she drank might someday kill her."

—

About two weeks later, the phone rang in the Zimmerman apartment. "Angelina, this is Jean-Paul."

"Ha! If I don't know your voice by now, I never will. What's happening?"

"I wanted you to know that I just received Elena's ashes from Campbell's Funeral Home. The box that we chose is perfect. Do you want me to bring it to you?"

"No, Jean-Paul. If you don't mind I'd rather you kept it in your home with Helen Dawson's remains. I really can't face it right now. But tell me, why don't you two come over at six o'clock so Gregorio and I can show you how much of the apartment has been cleaned up?

You won't recognize it. Then we can all go out to dinner. How does that sound?"

"Great! We'll be there at six. Do you have any booze or should we bring some champagne so we can have a drink before going out?"

"Sounds wonderful. By the way, I'm going back home to California the day after tomorrow. Gregorio will stay and see about the sale of the apartment. Harry was right. It's now worth around thirty million dollars.

"Oh, and another thing. I almost forgot to tell you that Carlo called this morning and asked about buying another apartment in this building. He must be crazy! They didn't steal that much money from my mother."

"No! But they would've if they could've! See you later."

~

It already looked like a different apartment when Jean-Paul and Christopher arrived that evening. Everything was spotless. They could once again see themselves in the mirror as they stepped out of the elevator. Although the apartment was still somewhat bare, Gregorio and Angelina had done their best to fill in the empty spots. And it was a pleasure to see the porcelain de Sévres back in the vitrines where they belonged.

Paintings that had been rescued from closets and storage bins were placed strategically to make up for the ones that were still missing.

It hadn't taken much to restore the library to its original glory, since the eighteenth-century boiserie was still magnificent. The furniture, beautiful as it was, paled by comparison.

It did seem odd, after all this time, to find the dining room without garbage and porcelain spread helter-skelter over the entire table. The paintings in the room were intact and, as in the old days, illuminated by pin spots that had been set in the ceiling.

Gregorio stood in front of the Empire breakfront, admiring the scene at the racetrack that had been painted by Raoul Dufy.

"By the way," he said, "we got a call the other day from Los Angeles to say that Carlo and Bea had forgotten two pieces of luggage at the airport. Then this morning, Hertz called to say that the car they rented at the airport has never been returned. On top of that, Carlo gave them the wrong area code for their home phone in L.A. But the most disturbing thing of all is that a company would allow a ninety-one-year-old senile man to drive one of their cars. I guess Bea must have done most of the talking!"

The last time Jean-Paul and Christopher had seen Bea and Carlo's rooms was right after the Manzianos had gone back to California. As the two men walked down the hallway, they were most curious to see how Angelina and Gregorio had managed to transform the nightmarish rooms back to the way Elena had originally decorated them.

"Hey," exclaimed Jean-Paul, awestruck, "I had forgotten how beautiful these rooms once were. The furniture in Bea's bedroom is even nicer than I remember. The Louis XVI bed and dresser are magnificent. I can see that the fabrics on the walls and the matching drapes are pure Elena. You certainly inherited her taste, Angelina. And Carlo's study/bedroom is really smart with the red leather on the walls and the modern bookcases. Many of the books are beautiful too. Before, it was hard to see them through all the mess. But how did you two ever get rid of that disgusting smell?"

"Not easy," answered Gregorio, "but it was mainly a matter of getting rid of the filthy bedding and old, unwashed clothes."

Angelina, who was rightfully proud of the strong stomach that had allowed her to clear out the rooms, chimed in. "There was one thing, though, that didn't make any sense. As you know, there were tons of junk piled everywhere—that is, everywhere except in her bedside table. I opened the drawer and pulled out an envelope that had been carefully hidden in the back. It was so well placed that even I almost missed it. I got such a creepy feeling when I pulled it out, that I ran to the bathroom and flushed the contents down the toilet."

Jean-Paul's antennae immediately went on alert as he asked, "What on earth did you find in this envelope?"

"Pills," answered Angelina. "Little white pills."

When Jean-Paul heard this, his stomach nearly rolled over. He had to sit down before he passed out from the shock. He had never gotten over the fear he had felt when Marlene had first told him about the "little white pills" that Bea had repeatedly tried to force the aides to give to Elena.

"Jean-Paul, What's the matter? You're pale as a ghost."

Christopher, who understood the implications of what Angelina had just said, sat next to his partner and gently put an arm around his shoulder.

"Angelina, is it possible that you have any of the pills left, or even the envelope?" asked Christopher.

"No, of course not. I threw everything out that day. I didn't want any of her things left in the house. What is this all about?"

Jean-Paul explained carefully about Bea and the little white pills.

Gregorio said, "So now there's no way to test the pills to find out for sure if that's what killed her. And in the end, Elena only left them five hundred thousand dollars—a pittance compared to what they had planned on getting away with."

CHAPTER 25

Six months after Elena's death, Gregorio sold his grandmother's apartment for thirty million dollars. He had been a huge comfort to Angelina, not only emptying the apartment, but also taking care of all the business aspects of the Zimmerman estate.

He was now a very rich young man with the financial means to pursue his dream, which was to cultivate a vineyard in Italy; and he would be able to fly to his mother at a moment's notice if her fragile health should suddenly deteriorate.

But he had one more task on his agenda before he could close the book on his grandmother's estate: his work would not be done until he made a trip to visit Carlo and Bea at their home in a suburb of Los Angeles.

Jean-Paul and Christopher were visiting Angelina then, at her home in San Marino. When she told them that Gregorio would arrive soon, and what he planned to do, they couldn't wait to see him and hear the details.

Many times Jean-Paul had pleaded with him, "Gregorio, if nothing else, you have to at least drive by Carlo and Bea's house and let us know what it's like. No one has ever been allowed to see it. And if you can get inside, it would be even better. Maybe you'll find some of the things that they stole from your grandmother over the years. In any case, at least give me a report on what it looks like from the outside."

At last the time had come. Gregorio, too, was intrigued about the state of their home, but he also had a mission to accomplish.

On his way from the Los Angeles airport, he tried to call the Manzianos. There was no reply. But then again, they never answered the phone. The only option he had left was to show up unexpectedly on their doorstep.

The first thing he noted was that the neighborhood was run down and probably had seen better days. The house itself fit in perfectly with the surrounding area. The paint was peeling off the sides and the roof looked about to cave in at any moment. There was not a live bush, flower or blade of grass to be seen anywhere.

As he got out of the car and walked up the broken pathway to the front door, Gregorio thought, This looks like Death Valley!

There was no response when he carefully stepped on what was left of the front porch and called out, "Hello, is anybody home?"

When he tried the handle of the front door, he was surprised to find it open. How bizarre that two people who had lived behind closed doors for so many years should now leave the front door of their house unlocked.

"Hello," he cried out again as he stepped inside.

Facing him was a wall of packing boxes with two narrow paths—one going to the kitchen and one leading to the bedroom. From one side came a little old man dressed in faded slacks and a torn sweater.

"Could this be my Uncle Carlo?" wondered Gregorio.

At the same time, a woman squeezed through the packing boxes on the other side of the room. The first thing he noticed was long white hair that hung down to her shoulders. She was once again wearing Elena's favorite black velvet Valentino evening gown, which she had appropriated the night Elena died. By now, the velvet was worn through in places and the dress was covered with multiple unidentifiable spots. On the fourth finger of her left hand was the copy of Elena's thirty-carat diamond ring. Cheap costume jewelry adorned her wrists, while black grime mixed with old makeup was evident in the folds of Bea's aging neck.

These two people had deteriorated so rapidly since Elena's death, that the most recognizable thing about them was the odor of decay that Gregorio remembered all too vividly from their quarters in Elena's apartment.

"Young man," cried out Bea as she rushed to embrace him, "what a pleasure. I wish we could ask you to sit down, but we haven't yet had a chance to unpack everything. Welcome to our home. It's so good to be back in our own place again. Isn't this a lovely house?"

"Yes, Bea, it's very nice," replied a stunned Gregorio.

"Just wait until we redo everything. Maybe we'll call in the same decorator who did such a beautiful job on Elena's apartment. Of course, moving back to our old apartment building in New York is not out of the question either. We have so much to do now. Isn't that right, old man?

"God help me, I don't know why I keep him around. He's more trouble than he's worth. All he does from morning to night is stand around shaking his head back and forth, back and forth, just like those stupid dolls people stick in the back window of their cars. Believe me, I could do a lot better than him. I could have men lined up around the corner waiting for me to give them a chance. Of course, I have to organize this place first. But I have to do it all myself. That stupid, stupid man is no help at all. Are you, you old fool?"

Gregorio almost felt sorry for his ninety-two-year-old uncle, who could do nothing but stare at the eighty-eight-year-old woman while she tore him apart and called him ugly names.

"Yes, I think it's about time that I got rid of him. After all, I'm still young, beautiful, and rich, with a whole life ahead of me. Or maybe I should just get a young lover. Yes that's it, a young lover. After all, that old fool hasn't been of any use for years. Have you, old man?"

Gregorio could have sworn that she fluttered her overly made up eyelashes at him when she talked about taking on a young lover. The whole scene was getting far too uncomfortable, and he was beginning to regret having ever walked into this insane world of fantasy.

"Uhm, I'm going to have to leave in a few minutes, but I brought a piece of paper with me that has to do with my grandmother's estate. I wonder if your husband could sign it for me."

"Of course, you adorable young thing. Whatever you want is yours," answered Bea with a broad wink that left little to the imagination.

Gregorio decided that he might as well play along for the moment, until he got what he had really come for.

"Go ahead, sign the paper, you old fool!" barked an impatient Bea.

Carlo looked around in bewilderment and said, "But I need a table to write on."

"Then let's go into the kitchen. We have a table there. Then I can show this lovely young man the rest of our beautiful home," offered Bea with a sly, meaningful glance that almost brought Gregorio to the brink of a panic attack.

"Here you go," said Gregorio. "Why don't you use this packing box as a desk? It's much easier than having to go all the way into the kitchen. I have a pen, so we're all set."

Neither Carlo nor Bea asked one question about the paper that they were signing. Carlo was too overwhelmed and confused, while Bea's only thought was of getting the good-looking visitor into her filthy bed for a playful romp. It was never clear to Gregorio if either of the old folks knew or even cared who he really was.

As soon as Carlo had signed the document, Gregorio started making his way towards the front door. "Gee, thank you for everything. I hope to see you both soon. It's been a pleasure."

Gregorio was out the door before either Carlo or Bea could react to his departure. Clutched in his hand was the document that Carlo had just signed, renouncing the Manzianos' rights to the half million dollars Elena had left them in her will. Racing to his car, Gregorio could hear loud voices from inside the house.

"You stupid, stupid man! It's your fault that he ran away like that. You ruin everything, you old fool."

"Shut up, Bea. I've had enough of your telling me I'm stupid. I don't want to hear it anymore!"

Bea, whose decades of greed and jealousy and desire to be Elena had finally sent her over the edge and into a world of total madness, shrieked, "It's not Bea anymore. Remember the little white pills? Remember Dr. Jonas and the injection? She's dead. Now I'm Elena!"

The next thing Gregorio heard was a crash and the sound of boxes falling to the floor, then a meek little voice that said, "Yes, Elena."

—

The real Elena had been given so many "gifts" in her lifetime. Jean-Paul had always believed that if you are given wealth and fame, extraordinary beauty, or a great talent, it is not a gift but rather a test. Someone in the great beyond is looking down and saying, "Now, what are you going to do with it?" In the end, Elena's gifts had become a tragedy of riches.

Tony Cointreau, a member of the French Cointreau liqueur family, was born into a life of wealth and privilege, growing up among the rich and famous. His maternal grandmother was an opera star, and Tony's own voice led him to a successful international singing career. His paternal heritage put him on the Cointreau board of directors. But he felt a need for something more meaningful in his life—and his heart led him to Calcutta and Mother Teresa. In her last letter to Tony, Mother Teresa wrote, "You are the sunshine of love."

www.tonycointreau.com